The collection My Truth My Story comprises a dozen short stories written by Gayatribala Panda originally in Odia and excellently translated into English by Snehaprava Das, a noted translator of Odisha. Firmly grounded in reality the stories narrate the plight of the common man caught in the dilemma between the sublime and the trivial. Gayatribala's etching of characters continue to haunt us long after the stories are read. I would think that this volume is an important addition to the gamut of Indian Literature.

- Nirmalkanti Bhattacharjee
*An accomplished translator from Bengali into English
and vice versa, and Editor of Niyogi Books*

My Truth My Story is a heartwarming collection of twelve Odia short stories by Gayatribala Panda translated ably in English by Snehaprava Das. The sheer variety of themes Gayatribala engages with, the brilliance of treatment and the pathos and compassion of the author set this collection apart.

- A.J. Thomas
Poet, translator, and former editor of Indian Literature

Although the stories in this collection take place in the background of Odishan villages, they make us deeply aware of how the minds of the inner villages of India are beating and what their lives are like. Hence these stories have a national character.

-Benyamin
Famous Novelist and short story writer in Malayalam

My Truth My Story

My Truth My Story

Gayatribala Panda

Translated by
Snehaprava Das

Black Eagle Books
DUBLIN, USA | BBSR, INDIA
2022

Black Eagle Books
USA address:
7464 Wisdom Lane
Dublin, OH 43016

India address:
E/312, Trident Galaxy, Kalinga Nagar,
Bhubaneswar-751003, Odisha, India

E-mail: info@blackeaglebooks.org
Website: www.blackeaglebooks.org

First International Edition Published by
Black Eagle Books, 2022

My Truth My Story
by **Gayatribala Panda**
Translated by **Snehaprava Das**

Original Copyright © Gayatribala Panda
Translation Copyright © Snehaprava Das

Cover : **Prakash Mohapatra**
Interior Design: Ezy's Publication

ISBN- 978-1-64560-311-5 (Paperback)
Library of Congress Control Number: 2022945226

Printed in the United States of America

Translator's Note

Translation is an act of trust. It is a commitment to the trusting readers having little or no knowledge of the language in which the original work is written to gift them a parallel text which will evoke an identical response. It is some sort of a pledge of unswerving loyalty to the author of the original work. Translation is the act of capturing the right mood of the original and work out the right mode of its transference to the replicated version. Easier said than done ! Because all these commitments makes translating an extremely tricky task. So what happens when one sets out to translate Gayatribala Panda's Odia stories in English? The commitment of faithful replication and the need of transferring the aesthetic appeal to the translated version keep the translator precariously poised on the fulcrum, striving hard to keep the two texts balanced, and maintain equilibrium. While rendering the nuances typical to the culture-specific Odia language in English it is hardly possible to maintain a blind loyalty to the original and still make a claim that the English version will evoke an almost similar response from the non-Odia readers. Because a literal translation, while preserving the author's wordings, loses the nuances of the original while a free translation can capture more of these nuances, although it is, in fact, a rewriting of the original. Because a literal translation can reduce the translator, to quote H.W. Longfellow.. '.. to a witness called to a trial', who 'should be compelled to raise his hand and swear to tell the truth and nothing but the truth.'

The translator, in such cases rather should play the role of the one who, in the words of the Noble laureate German novelist Gunter Grass, 'transforms everything so that nothing changes.' Hence transforming Gayatribala Panda's stories the way Grass defines the act, becomes an experience of its own kind since they are stories that narrate the common incidents occurring in a common man's life in a conversational tone. They do not make any effort to transport the reader to the lofty heights of some sublime experience rather they keep him firmly grounded in reality. The author does not waste words in elaborate and exaggerated narration nor is she much inclined to probe into the depths of human subconscious, to explore the subliminal. She creates situations and characters which we find familiar and are easy to identify ourselves with. Her stories are set both in a town or a city and as well as a village. If her villages have the semblance of an urban ambience, her towns and cities are painted with a rural shade. The frequent interfacing of city-centric experiences and the sentiments of village life lends her stories their special and unique charm.

Stories like WITCH and THE CLAW foreground the social evils like pasting a label of a witch on an issueless woman and the exploitation of poor and helpless children by coercively engaging them in several criminal and illegal activities. WITCH is a bold attempt to expose the hypocrisy of people enjoying a respectable social status who try to derive a savage delight at the suffering of innocent human beings in the name of preservation of morals values, while THE CLAW unfolds a realistic picture of the gruesome details of the way a child trafficking racket operates.

A SONG FOR A SLAUGHTERER centres round the tragic life of the protagonist Karim who has entered into the meat-selling vocation more by default than by choice, and his futile effort to hide his woe under a fake joviality. Acute poverty, desertion by his disloyal wife and the accidental death of his two kids that followed her elopement with another man had left nothing in Karim's life to go on. He sacrifices his apparently 'not worth-living' life to save the kid son of one of his favourite customer(the narrator of the story) from being run over by a truck. The author has worked on the symbiosis of 'defeated by life' and 'defeating life' with the expertise of a seasoned story teller to make Karim's character appear larger than life.

BLACKIE is another moving and poignant tale of the love between a human child and a puppy. A mother with a deep-rooted aversion for dogs was forced rather by an emotional need to see her only son happy, to shelter a stray dog in the garage of her house. The female stray dog delivers a pack of puppies from amongst which the smallest, the weakest and the blackest turns out to be her son's most favourite. But it becomes too much of an effort for her to bear the presence of the 'abominable' creatures and one day while her son is out at school and her husband is on an official tour she bribes one of her trusted servants to carry away the puppy (her son calls it Blackie) in a gurney sack and leave it at the outskirts of the town from where it cannot find its way back to their house. But the puppy as it was let out of the sack follows the man in a frantic effort to get back to its home and gets run over by an oncoming truck. The boy who thinks Blackie, for some reason he cannot guess, has run away makes a desperate search for the puppy that yields no result. The shock and trauma of losing someone he was so fond of takes its toll on the boy's tender mind and he develops a difficult psychotic condition to the utter dismay of his mother, now torn with guilt and mortification.

THE WHITE CROW is in a way an attempt to explore the subconscious through the creation of a dream sequence. A collage of delusive images are etched out with the skill of a painter to project the repressed wishes of a woman who had secretly aspired to become a writer but was restrained from pursuing her goal because of her domestic encumbrances.

FIRE FESTIVAL unravels the ugly and reprehensible caste-discrimination prevailing in the society. It also exposes the brute sadism in man often kept concealed under a veneer of civility. It is a tragic tale of a crippled young man of a lower caste who was thrown alive into the raging fire by a bunch of boys of higher caste families. During the celebration of the annual fire festival the boys, acting under the influence of alcohol, throw Banshi, a crippled young boy of the village into the flames for sheer fun of it. The police come to investigate but apparently fail to find enough evidence to pin the crime on the culprits. The inspector conveniently concludes that Banshi, in a state of drunkenness had entered into the fire and was burnt to death. He registers it as an unnatural death in the official record and closes the case.

The dramatic and eerie beginning of the story BRAMHA-DEMON that hints at the reality of the uncanny presence of some discontented spirit actually develops to be the tale of an illicit love affair between a Brahmin young man, the spoilt son of a wealthy landlord of the village and a lower caste woman Sushie who happens to be the wife of Daiya, a farmhand employed by his father. An unexpected turn of events leaves the Brahmin young man an orphan and compels him to depend on the loyalty of that very farmhand. Later he leaves his house and farmlands in charge of Sushie and her husband Daiya and comes to settles in Bombay, but his ribaldry takes a heavy toll on him and he was identified HIV positive. The hospital in which he was getting treated sends him back to his native village. But the people of the village, on learning about the dreaded disease he suffers from, vehemently demand his exile. It was only Sushie, the farmhand's wife who he had had an affair with, lets him in and takes care of him. The man dies a peaceful death in her arms. No one was ready to touch his body or carry him to the village crematory ground and give him a decent funeral. Sushi boldly faces the resistance of the hostile villagers and cremates his body in the backyard of the house.

GRANDFATHER'S NOTEBOOK narrates the tale of a young girl sentenced to a lifelong remorse for not being able to fulfil the dying wish of her beloved grandfather who had to compromise with his writing career for providing a living to his family. Driven by acute poverty the man had to sell away the manuscripts of his novels to other people who got them published in their own names and were acknowledged as writers. The girl accidentally discovers one old manuscript which was actually her grandfather's autobiography. She shows it to her grandfather who struck by a paralytic attack, lies helpless and immobile in his bed. He entrusts his granddaughter, who he believes, has the unmistakable streak of a creative writer in her character, the responsibility of getting the book published in his own name. The girl promises her grandfather that she would fulfil his wish. He dies shortly after. The girl too comes to stay in the school hostel in order to prepare for her school finals. When she returns home after her examination, she discovers, to her utter dismay that her aunt has sold away the bulky manuscript along with the newspapers and other old books and magazines, to the scrap vendor.

THE DEAL is the story of Debadutta, a low-paid correspondent in a newspaper office and his difficult dilemma. An honest newspaper correspondent and a young man of self-esteem Debadutta falls victim to the evil designs of his corrupt and manipulating boss. Poverty and his mother's illness force him to acquiesce to the unfair proposition of the MD of the newspaper company much against his better judgments. The story outlines the pathetic predicament of the protagonist belonging to the lower middleclass segment of the society who gets caught in the grip of malicious and disagreeable circumstances and is compelled to compromise with his conscience.

VICTORY MARCH tells us about a man's goading passion to retrieve his ancestral property from the clutches of his greedy and hostile relatives. He wastes an entire lifetime and a good part of the money he has earned in fighting court cases to accomplish his purpose. He finally wins the case but realises that what he has lost while pursuing his aim was much more precious. He has lost his peace of mind, the happiness of spending time with his family and many such things which do not seem to have much material value but count a lot in our life. To fall a victim to our own compelling wishes is perhaps the biggest irony of human life.

An unexpected text message brings the bitter memory of a past episode back to life in THE FACE OF YESTERDAY. A forgotten love story comes alive fresh and vivid in her mind and so too her deep seated resentment for the man of her past who she had decided to share her future with but who had abandoned her without a strong or valid reason when Suman receives a text message from him on her mobile phone at the late hours of a night.

MY TRUTH MY STORY assails the despicable and unhealthy custom of polyandry that still prevails in some parts of the country. A reader, at times, may feel tempted to discern here the faint semblance of a myth that was given an appropriate twist of contemporaneity. The story exposes the evils of the selfish and rigid conditions designed by a gender biased society that reduce the status of a woman to a living object used to satisfy the libidinal urge of man. Very few men care to probe into the depth of a woman's mind to know and respect her wishes and aspirations. In all ages from ancient to modern a woman is forced to live this 'truth' which turns her life to an episode of agony.

While rendering stories like these with a strong flavour of Odianess in English the translator cannot claim that the English text is the same as the one in original Odia because it is an admitted truth that the same text cannot exist in two different languages. Despite the translator's sincere commitment to reproduce the original without any change, the text in English turns out to be a different one, the 'Other Text'. There is of course no noticeable change either in the subject matter or the sentiment embedded in it, but certainly this Other Text, as Gunter Grass points out, is a transformed text. Jacques Derrida rightly points out that 'If the translator neither copies nor restores the original it is because this survives and becomes something else.' 'The translation,' he adds, 'in fact becomes a moment in its own evolution, and the original is fulfilled even as it grows within the translation.' The original work, indisputably, grows in the translation. It acquires a freshness, a new dimension, a polish and an exotic flavour that add to its beauty. The stories in this collection, with these added elements, I believe will appeal to the aesthetic taste of both the Odia as well as the non-Odia readers.

Snehaprava Das

Contents

My Truth My Story

Every story holds a truth in it.
Every truth could be told as a story.
My story too holds my truth in it.
In fact my story is my truth!!
The wound still burnt mildly, over and over. Last night's wound... but hurt still, like a light sting from a poisonous prick. It had not left any noticeable mark anywhere though so that one can put a finger at the exact point where it hurts. Bearing the pain of a wound regularly is, in a way, becomes a normal act like suckling a baby, putting vermilion powder in the partings of the hair, or opening yourself up layer by layer in the dark of the night!

They couldn't see it. My four husbands, my old ma-in-law nor my three children did even have the slightest inkling of its existence. They, in their own respective ways, exercised their respective rights on me. Ma-in-law demanded nursing, the children needed caring, and my husbands demanded the quelling of their libido. None had time, nor had the inclination to inquire or know what I wanted. For ones like me, not the denial of the monstrosity of a custom but a resigned submission to it becomes the destiny.

Narendra, used to get literally transmuted to a wild

beast when his turn came to share a night with me. He mauled my body, each part of it with a savage curiosity as if he tried to discover something special. I often lay plastered to the bed like a smothered dollop of clay in the mornings after. Dorjee, the youngest of my four husbands was only twenty. It was but natural for a young man of his age to have more of that erotic interest in my body than anyone else. He never let go an opportunity of letting his eager exploring hand rove over the secret areas of my body. But my eldest husband Dharma found Dorjee's desire for me abhorring and unbearable. Given the slightest occasion he snapped at Dorjee. My intimacy with Dorjee sparked a fire of rage in him.

But Karma is different from his brothers. He did not seem to have that fire in him. Even when alone with me in the night, he was like a block of ice, frigid, calm and unmoved. But I understood him better than others because he never hid his feelings from me. But Dharma could make a guess. He could sense the intense love and respect I had for Karma. He got more and more aggressive each passing day. His bitterness for Karma kept growing interminably.

It was Karma who, at the age of eighteen, had defied this despicable custom.

'How can all of us four brothers marry one woman?' he had protested. 'But this is our tradition,' my ma-in-law explained. My ma-in-law had six husbands, and her ma-in-law had three. She had tried to reason it out to her son. But Karma was not convinced till the end. He had not touched me though he had married me under pressure. His mind was filled with Nima, his childhood friend. But she too had to submit to the wish of her people and marry in a family of seven brothers. How could a woman survive the torment of spending nights with seven husbands in turns? Nima committed suicide two years after her marriage. Karma was caught in the web of a terrible despair. The shock of the separation from Nima and her death filled him with such a grief that he found living a meaningless exercise. Time and life rolled along the charted route but the void which Nima's death had made in his heart was never filled again.

Dharma, Narendra and Dorjee spent their nights with me even when I was in the carrying stage. My pain and discomfort did not make any impact on their conscience. They would rather try to make the maximum of the nights that came in their share. It was only Karma who objected. 'How could you enjoy a woman in her condition? Are you monsters?' he used to say. But my ma-in-law countered. 'What is the harm in that?' she argued. 'They are men after all! It is good that they could derive all the pleasure they needed at home, from their own wife and do not have to go searching for it outside. That would have been disastrous for the unity of the family. That might lead to divisions of the home and the family property and many such complicated issues.'

To tell the truth, I was getting more and more inclined towards Karma. Narendra was the strongest , handsomest and most passionate among all four. Dharma had the expertise in the art of lovemaking. Dorjee was the youngest and exciting. He was never satiated yet got easily tired through the act.

But Karma dwelt in the bottom of my heart. My ma-in-law could guess it.

'Women like us are not destined to have a single husband,' she explained. 'The unity of the family will collapse unless you know how to share your love equally amongst all your husbands. The brothers will turn enemies of one another. The very purpose of the one-wife custom will be defeated.'

'You are the wife of all four of us,' Dharma too tried to explain. ' You must love all of us equally. You must divide your commitments and your love in equal measures amongst all of us. Yes, as the eldest of the brothers my claim on your love and on your time should be a more than others. No one else could exercise more right on you except me. I do not approve of the way you tilt towards Karma.' There was a mild yet unmistakable warning in his tone.

It was but natural that the brothers had occasional row over their rights and claim over me. They were jealous of the one other and secreted a doubt and a grudge against one another too. But they knew better than to let it surface. The image of the family and its décor were always prioritized.

A long time after my eldest son was born I could not be sure who his father was. He seemed to have taken after me. People said that a son whose looks resembled that of his mother was lucky. But that did not answer my question or satisfy my curiosity. The daughter that came next put me in a similar state of confusion. I looked closely at her face at times to decide who she actually looked like. Sometimes her face seemed to resemble that of Narendra while at others it looked more or less like Dorjee's. My ma-in –law said that she took after her grandfather. Her remark hit me like a knife- stab. But her eyes held no regret or remorse when she said it. She was rather exceptionally fond of the baby girl.

A few drops of secret tears trickled down my eyes. A stiff sob that remained stuck in me melted and disappeared into some dark labyrinth of my heart. But the sight of the little girl never failed to bring the sordid memory of that terrible incident back to my mind. The hairs on my body bristled in abject hatred and revulsion as I recollected it.

This was how it happened.

It was the sixth day of my regular monthly period. I had taken a head bath and sat in the verandah drying my hair in the sun. In the pot which I had put on the cooking hearth rice had begun to boil.I had bathed my eldest son, fed him and put him to sleep in the cloth-swing. All my four husbands were away at their respective work-places. Ma-in-law had gone to attend a sermon-preaching event.

A hand caressed my hair. Startled, I jumped to my feet and turned to look. May be one of my husbands, I thought. But no, it was my father-in-law who stood behind me. A fierce, all-consuming desire flamed in his hungry eyes. I struggled to free myself from his grip. But he was too strong for me.

'You are satisfying the demands of all four of my sons. What is the harm if there is one more addition to the list?' he sounded brazen and hoarse. 'You should rather feel happy that you could bring some pleasure to a man of my age.'

His voice was cool and casual as if he was not asking me my body but something like rice or dal or tea or snacks to slake his hunger. It was as ordinary as asking me to give him the tablet for his blood pressure or for his gastric complaint. I stared at him blankly my mind failing to register the vile reality of the situation. Without waiting for me to say anything he dragged me to one corner of the lonely verandah and committed the most heinous act a man is capable of committing. In that dark noon he played the flesh-game with me and won it despite all my efforts to resist him. When he finally got to his feet, satisfied, triumphant beads of perspiration glistened on his face.

I trembled in shame and fear. A loathing for my father-in-law which I have not felt for anyone till then combined with a sense of self-pity corroded me to the core. How was I going to look in the face of my ma-in-law and my four husbands after this?

Ma-in-law returned. I narrated the tale of my misery to her, my voice choking, copious tears running down my eyes.But there was no serious reaction.

'The libidinal urge of a man did not take either age or prudence into consideration.' She replied with her usual nonchalance. ' It is a woman's destiny to cater to all the needs of a man. She should think herself fortunate if she could give herself away to satisfy the men in her family.'

There was nothing more to complain about after this. There was no one to blame too, neither my destiny , nor a god if there was any, and not even my husbands!!

Things would have been left at that had it not been Karma's turn to spend that particular night with me.

And on that night there was a deviation in the usual pattern. Normally I came to the room after dispensing with the routine domestic chores of the night. As such Karma never touched me. He would be asleep by the time I came to the room.

It did not happen that way on that night. I was sobbing my heart out in to the pillow when Karma entered the room and closed the door. I had come to the room soon after serving the meal to the family members. I desperately needed the solitude of my room to release the pent up agony I had kept buried inside me all through the day. I needed the solitude to salvage the bits of my womanhood that was blown away in a series of explosions that battered my insides as I went about my routine works through the day. I needed to be left alone with myself for some time to put the pieces of that shattered womanhood at place and make it a whole once again.I had come to my room to let the scalding lava of the abomination flow away and get lost in the dark oblivion of that solitude.

As I said, the whole episode would have been put to rest without any fuss had it not been Karma's turn that night. As I lay weeping my heart out he stepped into the room and locked the door from inside. He turned to look at me and stopped short. It was an unexpected sight for him. He sat by me on the bed and wiped away my tears with tender hands. I was surprised. He had never touched me in all these years. There was something euphoric about the touch. It was almost enlivening, like that magic touch which had lifted the curse off Ahalya and changed her back to a woman. The touch sent a blissful shiver running into my veins.

My four husbands during their respective nights with me never had let go of the chance of clawing and mauling my body. It was not love but a legally sanctioned act of vilifying a woman. Their touch had never lifted me to this state of ecstatic bliss which the gentle hands of Karma did.

I was torn between two overwhelming yet contradictory emotions, between the intense joy which stirred in me with the gentle touch of Karma and the fierceness of the revulsion at the memory of the monstrosity with which my womanhood was defiled a few hours ago. Uncontrollable sobs rocked my body once again. Even as I struggled with my prudence I unfolded the gruesome story of the sacrilege before Karma, layer by layer. It was an inadvertence on my part—done without any intention. But it made a devastating impact on Karma. It made him fly into a mad rage. I had never seen him so angry during all these years. Without stopping to listen to my feeble protests, he rushed out of the door and stormed into my father-in-law's bedroom. Before anyone could guess what was happening

Karma pulled my father-in-law out of the bed and shoved him against the wall in an insane impulse. The back of his head hit the wall with great force. He was dead before he reached the hospital. There was a postmortem done by the hospital authorities since it was not a natural death. My ma-in-law had made all efforts to suppress the truth and make it pass as an accident but the hospital people were not convinced. The case was reported to the police. Dharma, the eldest of my husbands, and who had always nurtured a grudge against Karma testified against his brother. Karma too admitted that he had killed his father. He had no remorse for what he had done, rather he repeatedly told that what he had done was absolutely right. Death was the right punishment sinners like his father deserved.

The court gave its verdict and Karma was sentenced to long years of imprisonment.

' You must not feel sorry for me', Karma told me before he was sent to serve his stretch. 'That sinner had to be punished. I am rather happy that justice was done to you. Do not ever weep after this. I cannot see you in tears.'

'I cannot see you in tears...'

This one sentence, though small, brought a great change to my life. It brought me back the will to live on which I seemed to have lost long since. It imbued into me a sort of resilience and a new strength to survive the adversities.

'I will wait for you my dear Karma!' A voice inside me hummed softly, secretly--- on and often.

I tried vainly to recollect the look in Karma's eyes on the day the court pronounced the life-for verdict on him. I could not look him in the eyes at that moment. My heart was unbearably heavy with unshed tears. The chocking sob that stuck inside me threatened to melt and overflow the edges of my own eyes that strove hard to hold them in check. Karma's imprisonment had turned me to a stone, inert and lifeless. Despite my resolve to face the challenges life brought me with my newfound strength of Karma's love, I felt desperately lost. An overpowering sense of guilt had taken me in its grip. Karma would not have been put behind the bars had I not let him see my tears that night! He would be living a free life had I not let the singe of the flame that burnt my womanhood that night, touch his kind and sensitive soul!! The honour and good name of my family too would have remained unsoiled.

Would it have been the right thing to do, not to let Karma know what had happened, I wondered.

But had I not done so my father –in-law would have tried to take advantage of every possible opportunity to repeat the act of sacrilege, to keep on battering and bruising me with his animal desire. It would have made no impact on anyone of the family except me. I would have been the only one crumbling down under the loadof that savagery.

'I cannot see you in tears...'

Those few words Karma had said just before he was taken away kept haunting me, urging me to go on. But my life took a different turn thereafter. My mother-in-law ceased to take me into confidence and maintained a calculated distance from me. The three husbands of mine, Dharma, Narendra and Dorjee went about their business in a mechanized pattern and exercised their ownership over my body in the nights as they had been doing over the years. Despite the normal routine it followed, life was plunged into a vacuum that kept on growing fast and non-stop.

I felt unusually lonely after Karma was sent to jail and the loneliness brought me back the vivid memory of

Rajiv, my childhood friend. I could clearly remember the waves of pain that rose and broke in his steady gaze the day on which I was given in marriage to the four brothers and was sent off to my in-law's house. The picture of those grim eyes heavy with unshed tears had remained stuck permanently in some hidden corner of my mind. There was something in that gaze which whenever returned to my memory pulverized me. Often in my lonely moments I was thrust into the cul-de-sac of the past where memories sauntered on together holding hands. I closed my eyes and they closed in on me, crowded me. I saw a pair of speaking, wet eyes gazing fixedly on me. Whose eyes were they? Rajiv's?Karma's?

Rajiv was my classmate and childhood friend. He was a sick boy and polio had crippled one of his legs. His family was poor and his widowed mother was a paraplegic too. I liked his innocence and sincerely sympathized with him. By the time my adolescent sympathy for Rajiv was transmuted to friendship and then to something more we both had stepped on the threshold of youth. Rajiv had begun to fill my youthful dreams. Despite the many factors that might not have gone in its favour I had started to nurture a secret wish to be his bride because Rajiv possessed an innocent, guileless heart. It was like a tranquil, beautiful sea and I wanted to spend endless hours on its solitary shore. But there was another strong and more practical reason that prompted me to marry Rajiv. He was the only son of his parents and marrying him would have spared me the humiliation and torments of being the wife of more than one husband. But neither destiny nor the circumstances seemed to stand by me. my eldest brother was exceptionally rigid in his objection to our marriage.

My mother had married two husbands and we were

six brothers and sisters of our two fathers. One of my fathers succumbed to the deadly disease of cancer. The other one fell a prey to tuberculosis and quit the mortal world soon after. The entire load of the responsibility of our family was shifted to the inexperienced shoulders of my eldest brother after the death of my fathers. Life had not been kind to him and the constant and difficult demands it made from him had turned my elder brother rude, impatient and irritable. It was only he, the eldest male of our family who had the prerogative of taking all decisions in everyone's behalf. My mother and my two married sisters were not against the marriage but women in our family had not had a say in such serious matters. Nor did they have the courage or position to protest my brother's decision. My sister-in-law, the wife of my three brothers had her hidden consent but she too preferred to maintain a discreet silence in this matter. She did not sincerely want me to live a life of divided womanhood like most women of our community and to be led to a pathetic ruin.

My brother might have been persuaded to consider Rajiv as a suitor for my marriage though it did not seem so easy, had not the tragic episode involving my second sister Tashi left its black, indelible mark on his heart. My elder sister Tara had married in a family of six sons. On every visit to our house she narrated the sordid tale of her life, the shame and humiliation of being the wife of six men. My second sister Tashi heard the grim tales with abject revulsion. Sometimes the grievances of Tara reached my eldest brother's ears, but he ignored them and explained to Tara that it is her duty to respect their custom and to put up with the inevitabilities. Every time she expressed her unwillingness to go back my eldest brother convinced Tara and made her to return to the house of her in-laws'.

But when she narrated the loathsome tale of how she was forced to sacrifice herself to the animal passion of six men in turns the blood that boiled in her erupted like lava and leaped out of her eyes to drown the world in its burning waves. The flame that smouldered in her eyes spread out like wildfire to consume the whole cosmos. The heat of her blazing abhorrence frightened us out of our wits. It made Tashi tremble in fear. I was, in a way, feeling a bit relieved. I was not destined perhaps, I hoped, to live through such hell since Rajiv was the only son in their family. But Tashi was full of apprehensions and wept her heart out in utter distress.

Finally Tashi's marriage was fixed. She was to go to a family of seven brothers. Tashi was heartbroken. Tara came and persuaded Tashi not to yield to such injustice. 'It is much better to run away or commit suicide,' she alerted her sister. But our eldest brother, to avoid complications, had fixed the marriage at a short notice without giving any one time for any detailed discussion or think of any suitable alternative.

The seven brothers and their relatives arrived at the bride's house in a ceremonial procession on the day of the marriage. But surprising all Tashi firmly declared her unwillingness to marry the seven grooms. The unexpectedness of the event stunned every one. It was as if a bombshell was dropped and the explosion that followed had sent everyone flying in bits out of their complacent corners. But Tashi was unmoved. The grooms' family demanded back the cash amount they had paid as the bride price. But my brother had spent quite a reasonable amount from it to meet the expenses of the marriage. He asked for some time to raise money for returning the amount to the grooms' family. But the insulted party remained stubborn on its demand. Soon the argument developed in to a serious confrontation and during the commotion that followed Tashi went into her room escaping the notice of all, and strangled herself.

The humiliation of not being able to return the money to the grooms' family combined with the disgrace of Tashi's suicide had made a serious impact on my brother. Tashi's death had shocked him no doubt, but everything put together had made him more aggressive and arrogant than before.

People in the village let their imagination run wild while picking up possible reasons of Tashi's suicide.There were hushed and disturbing whispers all around. A rumor that Tashi had got pregnant from a secret affair with somebody and committing suicide was the only alternative for her, travelled round the village and its neighbourhood. The disastrous consequences emerging from the fouled up plans of his sister's marriage and the slanderous remarks on her character had left my brother thoroughly shaken. He was becoming more and more bitter and rude.

When it came to his knowledge that I liked Rajiv, my brother had fixed my marriage in a family that lived at a far off place. He made it sure that the family of my in-laws' would under no circumstances come to know of the scandals involving Tashi's suicide. It was all so quick and so sudden that I had no time nor a chance to think of any escape-way. To sacrifice my dreams in the scaffold of my brother's decision was the only thing I could do to erase the dark spot on my dead sister's character and to prove that I had nothing to do with Rajiv. My brother had become so violent after learning my wish to marry Rajiv that I was afraid he might harm Rajiv in some manner, or even go to the extent of eliminating him if I did not agree to marry the grooms he had chosen for me.

He had strictly warned Tara not to make a visit to our house till my marriage ceremony was over. It had got into his mind that had it not been for Tara's provocations Tashi would never have taken such an extreme step. He was apprehensive that Tara might put some such thing in my mind too.

On the day of my wedding Rajiv had come to our house. He sought my brother's permission to meet me just for once. Though my brother gave the permission, he also remained present there. Rajiv could not say what he wanted to say to me in my brother's presence.

Rajiv's face was a blank mask of misery. The vacant look in his eyes reflected a total lostness. It made me feel I too was lost forever in a blind labyrinth. There was a strange calm in those eyes like the calm that settles after a storm. But I was not able to read his eyes correctly. Even after all these years the frustration of failing to decipher the meaning of that look in Rajiv'a eyes sent a stir of torment through me. I wondered at times if that was what had made me so resigned and indifferent towards my family.

Since that day I had neither met Rajiv nor had got any news of him. Often I felt curious to know if Rajiv had begun to learn to shape his life in the pattern society had set for him. Even when my life with my children and my husbands seemed to be moving smoothly in its ordained track, there were times when it got desperately stuck in the snare of such disturbing questions.

Time and again the face of Karma flashed before my eyes.

There was the same steady, fixed and more or less the same indecipherable gaze as that of Rajiv in that pair of serene eyes. I remembered his gentleness, his undemanding nature and the ease with which he had compromised with life. I got distracted whenever I remembered the look in Karma's eyes when I had seen the last of him. But my three husbands could never notice any change in me. Only Karma could sense when I felt distrait and lost. That was why perhaps I had had a tremendous weakness for Karma, I decided.

We three, Karma, I and Rajiv, were as though the three arms of a thick black triangle.

We were like three lost, floundering souls vainly groping for an intimate touch in that engulfing darkness.

It might be easy to bump against one another in the darkness, but difficult to touch one another closely.

This perhaps was the truth of our lives.

May be this truth could be told as a story.

There are times when life itself becomes a story.

Time drifted by. It was almost five years after Karma was sent to jail.I have become the mother of one more son, and still another life was beginning to germinate in me. The child that will be born would never know who its father was nor could I myself be sure of it. It could be any one, Dharma, Narendra or Dorjee! But I had stopped bothering because there was no need either for me or for the world to know or decide it.

Life would be unendingly racing on the blind track of time, and turning to a story at every lap.

In every sentence of that story Truth and Lie would be perpetually engaged in a game of hide and seek.

I would be trying to adorn those words and sentences with the sound of something smashing inside me rising to a crescendo.

Or, I would be dipping my brush at times in tear or in blood at others to paint the portrait of life with the theme of that story.

But still, I would be listening clearly the abuses the world would be flinging at me for going off track while narrating the tale of my truth.

●●

Blackie

It might not be easy to believe that an incident involving a puppy could set off such a complex chain of action. But it was the bitterest and the gloomiest truth that changed my life!

I had an inherent revulsion for dogs. I disliked cats too, but I was more allergic to the dogs. The degree of my distaste for the dogs could have been an interesting material for a story or even a novel. But I kept myself at a safe distance from the thought of writing on that. The moment I contemplated writing something on them the picture of dogs, lots and lots of them and of all possible breeds starting from the classy Dalmatian with which Priyanka Chopra did an ad, to the mangy stray bitch limping along the street in front of my house, sauntered in to the range of my vision. They all stood by my writing table in a row and began barking. The noise, like a knife-stab tore at my insides with a force that was almost diabolic.

God! What an abominable species! How horrifyingly savage!!

As though each one of them was salivating to lick my life away, year by year!

My, husband, on the other hand was very fond of dogs. Given a chance he would cradle it in his arms, play with it and let it sleep in his bed. He could even put it in his lap and drive it to the places he went on his official tour. The dog has to be of course cuddly and cute! But he never broached the subject openly since he knew how violent my reaction would be. So he tried to be mildly persuasive. He would keep counting the merits of a pet dog, its absolute faithfulness to its master, and the need of such a faithful animal to guard our big house. But my protests that came out in angry screaming every time he suggested keeping a dog as a pet did not allow the subject to develop into a healthy discussion.

'I think you have carried this hatred for dogs forward from some previous life!' he would say, his tone defeated and reconciling.

There were times when I too, was tempted to share his guessing.

When I was a child I had heard a strange episode relating to dogs. Someone in my village narrated a weird tale of a woman giving birth to a puppy. The woman that had delivered the baby dog, they said, was often complaining about a scratching pain in his womb when she was in the carrying stage.

A human giving birth to a dog!! Unthinkable and absurd!! But the tale had left a strong impact in my tender mind. How could a puppy enter the belly of a human being? The thought of a puppy entering a human belly filled me with such horror that the very sight of a dog repelled me. I could neither get rid of nor get over my hatred for dogs even at a much later age. Dogs never stopped frightening me.

The village street got packed with bunches of puppies during early winter. To me, even the thought of one female dog delivering nearly or more than half a dozen babies at one time was shocking. I wondered how so many baby dogs found their way to one mother dog's belly. Was the space in her belly wide enough to accommodate them all? Many of the puppies used to die at birth. The sight of a bundle of repulsive looking puppies swarming about the legs of a still more repulsive looking bitch was so detestable that I threw stones at them to drive them away. It felt as if the tiny ugly animals were crawling around my own legs. If there was a stick at hand I beat them unfeelingly. No one at my parent's home had any inclination for keeping pets, particularly dogs. My mother, however, used to dump the leftover food before the stray dog that lay crouched in front of our main gate most times of the day. She was not doing it as a compulsion. It was neither a routine nor my mother had any such interest in petting a dog.

I was not sure how much truth was there in that tale of a woman delivering a puppy, nor was there any possible scope or way to check its veracity. But the thought itself was venomous enough to turn me against all the dogs of the world.

The most despicable things about dogs that repelled me were their ominous whining that predicted some impending mishap, and their outrageously shameless fornication in the streets. My father had often asked me not to be superstitious about the mournful howling of dogs but I had my own arguments to support my belief. I remembered how a stray dog had whined all day and all night and soon after that my grandmother had died, all on a sudden.

How desperately I wished the species of dogs go extinct from the surface of the earth!!

I recollected the horrible experience of our Shilong trip. The trip had turned out to be a disaster on account of dogs. I had heard that the all hotels and restaurants there served dishes of pork and dog meat. We avoided hotels and stayed there with a professor in the Central University, an Odia. We carried with us fruits, bread and snacks during the sight-seeing programs. Flayed carcasses of dogs, pigs, and cows hung from hooks in the roadside meat shops. I could not bear to glance at them. The day on which we were on our way to Cherrapunjee, the vehicle we were travelling in had a break down in midway and we had to move into another car. My little son was crying hard and in that rushed moment of transferring our things to the second cab we forgot the lunch basket in the first cab. Finding no alternative we had to go into a hotel for lunch. But the hotel did not cater anything except non-veg item and the two specialities of the day were the dish of dog meat and pork. There was no other hotel in the vicinity for making a try. The smell of dog meat and pork cooking made my flesh creep. It was so nauseating that I ran out to the open and threw up. We had to remain without food the entire day. We dropped the programme of visiting Cherrapunjii and came back. I never stopped blaming the damned dogs thereafter. It was because of them our trip to Shillong had ended in a fiasco. My husband knew that my aversion to dogs had multiplied several times after that trip. Hence he never persuaded me to pet a dog.

But my kid son became excessively fond of the dogs. Whenever a dog came in sight, he ran to it and grabbed it in his tiny arms. He had no fear that the dog might scratch or bite him.

'Come here! Come here!' He would click his tongue and send a lisping invitation to every dog that passed by our house. Given the slightest chance he would cuddle it and to my horror, even kiss it.

My husband too had noticed his unusual attraction for dogs and one day brought a cute puppy home. I sulked the entire day.

'Can't you see how fond of dogs our son is!' He explained trying to assuage my anger. 'He is playing with the street dogs. There would always be the possibility of infections. Isn't it better to have a dog, vaccinated and healthy, of our own? Is your distaste for dogs more important than our son's happiness?' I had to accept his explanation much against my will since it was in the interest of our son.

But several questions cluttered in my mind and I wanted satisfying answers to them before giving my consent.

'It is so young. Who would look after it?' I asked.

'I will,' said my husband, sounding very convincing. 'I will take it away for a stroll, clean its wastes and bathe it.'

'You know our son is asthmatic. Haven't the doctors advised us not to go for pets?'

I was not ready to give in easily.

'These breed of dogs do not grow much fur.'

'I know! You have brought that animal because you have always wanted a pet dog, the interest of our son in dogs is just an excuse.' I said, heaving a sigh of defeat.

And the puppy lived with us in our house. My husband took all care of it as he had promised. I used to send it out to the balcony and close the door from inside when my husband went to office. The puppy yelped nonstop till he came from the office and opened the door to let it in. The sound of its barking rattled my nerves and I kept myself locked in my bedroom to shut noise out. I felt like a caged animal myself, confined within the four walls of my own house.

A week passed. And then it happened.

The blasted puppy cut the door curtains into shreds. It cut the sofa covers and pulled the stuffing out. I was insane with rage. My husband, afraid that the situation might take a more disastrous turn, gave away the puppy to one of his friends.

For a long time thereafter there were no discussions on the subject.

Everything was well and good till we came to live in our own house.

The place where we had constructed our new house could neither be called a town nor a village. This residential locality touched the outskirts of a village and the road that passed by the colony led straight off to the fringe of the village. More than few owners leased out their plots to the builders and lived in the main town. Not many people lived in the houses they had built. So the place was a little lonely. It had a peaceful rural ambience. The only snag about the place was the abundance of stray dogs. Because the place was not much populated dogs enjoyed an unbounded freedom here.

My son's love for dogs that had gone into dormancy surfaced itself after we came to live here. He stood hours on end in the balcony watching the dogs roaming in the street. I had no idea when and how he had brought the dog inside the compound until one day I discovered it settled cosily in one corner of our garage. Later I learnt that he was regularly giving food to that stray dog, and encouraged by my son's coaxing the dog had made a safe entry into our compound and from there to our garage. It was quite shocking but I could not hurt my seven year old kid's feelings. He called the dog Lali (it was a female dog), and spent hours playing with her. Lali, however, did not give me much reason to get upset with her. She remained out of the house during most parts of a day and returned only when it was time to eat. Our cook Raghu put the food out for her. Lali was a calm and quiet creature. She did not bark and growl without a reason like many other dogs but she would not let any stranger inside.

There were people who sneered at her. 'Look at her attitude!' They would say with a scoffing undertone. 'A bitch of native breed is she, but conducts herself like a Doberman or a Labrador!!'

Different people had different views on the issue.

'You must go for a healthy dog of a classy breed if at all you are keen on keeping a pet. This mangy stray bitch tells upon your social status.'

'Get rid of this sick creature, soon or your son might catch an infection.'

'These dogs of native breed are the most unscrupulous ones. They would eat at your home but go wagging their tails to keep guard over someone else's.'

It was not so that such remarks did not wound my sentiments, but to be honest, I did not hold any grudge against the poor animal because it never interfered in our life. I just ignored it and life went on apparently smoothly.

But on a fine morning my son ran into the house, dishevelled and panting, to declare that Lali was missing!

'I have searched at all possible places but she is nowhere!' Anxiety dripped from his voice.

This was my chance to motivate my son against keeping pets which I thought I must not let go.

'Now you know their nature, don't you? These ungrateful creatures are never to be trusted. I have explained it to you several times but you won't listen to me!'

'She was pregnant. Raghu uncle says.' My seven year

old son who looked crestfallen at the sudden disappearance of his pet dog countered me. 'He says that Lali has gone away to some secluded place to give birth to her puppies.'

So it was Raghu who taught all these things to my son, I thought angrily. But my better judgment prevented me from charging Raghu for such a simple matter.

Lali returned after a few days. She did not come inside the compound but whimpered crouching outside the front gate.

Raghu, my son at his heels, went to the front gate, opened it and let Lali in. then he put out some food on the plate Lali used to eat from. I watched it all from the balcony and quite surprisingly, I enjoyed the scene.

After sometime my kid son ran to me, breathless in excess of joy.

'Lali has come back mommy! My prayer is answered. I don't know how many puppies she has given birth to or where are they but I will find out and play with them.' His eyes sparkled in excitement as he said this.

I maintained a stony silence.

One evening as I was about to enter the house after returning from a meeting a flock of puppies crawled about my legs. Exasperated, I stepped into the front room quickly ant tried to shut the door on them. But they had already entered the room. My son, bubbling with joy ran into the room after them.

'They are Lali's puppies, mommy,' he announced effusively. 'One black, two white and two brown ----aren't they cute? The black one is the weakest of them. Raghu uncle had given it some milk. It needs to drink milk every day or else it will become weaker. This brown one gets angry easily and bites and scratches at its siblings at the slightest provocation.'

'Tell me something mommy,' he asked me, a serious look in his eyes. 'How do so many puppies remain together in the belly of one mother dog? Is there enough space in the mother dog's belly for them?'

I turned to look at the door. Raghu, our cook and my son's confidante stood there, smiling through his pressed lips. His amused smile poured oil in the flames of my anger.

'You are the central character in this dog-drama!' I burst out in anger. 'You are to be blamed for everything that is going on here. My son is just a kid. But you being an elderly and matured person are encouraging him to play with dogs! Disgusting! Get these horrors away from here immediately! '

Raghu did not say anything, nor did he try to offer any explanation. He shooed the puppies out of the room. But they did not go out of the compound. They squeezed in through the narrow gap under the gate as many times as Raghu pushed them out to the road.

The brown puppy bit three of its siblings to death within a few days. A car ran over another and crushed its legs, and it died soon after. Only two puppies, one white and another black, were left alive now. And after a few more days the white one went missing. It never returned. The weak and impoverished black puppy, the only survivor, remained with us. It was a mild natured dog like its mother Lali, and did not bark much. My son had named it Blackie. But I got mad with rage day I discovered that Blackie had cut all our footwear into pieces. Without pausing to think even for a moment I thrashed the puppy and its mother mercilessly with a stick and drove them out of the gate.

Tired and spent after all that exercise I walked back to the front room, flopped on the settee and breathed a sigh of relief. 'They will come back,' Raghu said.

'Yes,' I sniggered. 'Sure. It is because you people keep pampering and feeding them. Beat them hard if they try to come back. Put so much fear into them that they will never again try to get into our compound.' I looked at Raghu as I said this. He smiled mysteriously.

'You might exercise your authority over your son and over this house,' his smile seemed to say. 'But you can never keep the dogs under your control. You are not their master!'

I walked to my room without saying a word. My son looked sad and pale.

I went down to the compound in the evening to find the puppy and its mangy mother cosily sheltered in the garage.

'Didn't I tell you that they would come back?' Raghu said, a knowing look in his eyes.

The flame of frustration and defeat that flared inside me rose up to the sky. The heat smouldered and scorched me. But neither could I douse the flames myself nor could I seek any aid from anyone to do so.

I have to invent some new strategy, I decided. I was fighting a lone battle against my son, my husband, my cook and an army of dogs. They were not laced with any sharp weapons, nor were they attacking me. Their silent obduracy and small innocent smiles hit me at the very core of my being, and I was bathed in my own blood. I felt vanquished. No! I would not let myself be defeated by an obscure stray dog. I have to be diplomatic and conniving.

I looked again at them. My son poured out milk in a big bowl. He tore open the wrapper of a biscuit packet and put all the biscuits in front of the puppy. 'My Blackie was beaten hard today,' I heard him saying to Raghu. 'It needs good and healthy food. You must give it milk and biscuits regularly.'

I turned my face and walked away from the place. I have to get rid of this nuisance permanently. But how? How?

Then something happened which tore at the last straw of my patience.

A friend of mine who had settled abroad visited us. As we received him at the front gate my son came running to the place, his face lit up with a happy smile. The puppy and its mother followed him docilely. 'It is Lali, my pet dog!' he declared proudly. My guest cast a glance at Lali and smiled at my son.

'And the puppy? Is that your pet too?' He asked.

'Yes, the puppy too. It is called Blackie.'

I turned to look at the puppy. Sometime back someone had thrown hot gruel at it. Most of its fur was burnt away and the skin peeped out in ugly patches. Its ribcage was distinctly outlined under its parchment like skin. The contempt and repulsion in the eyes of my guest were like knife-slashes at my ego.

But my son took no notice of it. He went on narrating the episodes about how Lali and Blackie came to live with us. His face glowed as he went on speaking. My guest listened to him patiently. He probably did not want to hurt my son's sentiments. But my mind was busy in making plans to rid myself off this dog- trouble once and for good.

Two days after the incident of our friend's visit our cook Raghu took leave for a week and went to his village.

At last the opportunity I had been waiting for all these days was at hand! After my son went away to the school and my husband left for office I phoned to the man who worked as a temporary gardener for us and asked him to come to our house.

'Get a gunny sack,' I said giving him two hundred

rupees. 'Put this puppy inside it and take it away from here. Leave it at some far off place.'

The man was very happy to get two hundred rupees for a small job like this. He put Blackie in the gunny sack and carried it away on his bi-cycle.

'Where did you leave it?' I asked when he returned.

I had left him at the side of the *Bhuasuni* temple. But it trailed after me. A truck ran over it as it was trying to cross the road. Your problem is now permanently over,' he said expecting perhaps a few words of praise from me. I gave him another hundred rupees and warned him keep the matter secret. He went away happily with this unexpected bonus.

I did not feel very happy about the way things happened. A cloud of guilt hung heavy over my heart. The desperate yelping of the little dog and the mute agony in its mother's eyes haunted me the rest of the day. The poor mother dog had tried hard to stop the man from putting its baby in the gunny sack. It had run after the bicycle for quite a distance and finally gave up. It returned to the garage and wailed pitifully for some time and then went away. It never returned.

'Where are Lali and Blackie?' was the first question my son asked on returning from school.

'Might have been roaming somewhere,' I replied nonchalantly.

'Where ?' He was not ready to leave it at that.

'How do I know? They never told me where they were going!' I said and dismissed the topic.

My son flung his school bag at on the settee and went outside to look for the dogs. He returned after a while, his face clouded. 'They are nowhere here!' He said and began to cry. I solaced him and said that they would surely return.

He did not look very convinced. Had Raghu been there he would have asked him to make a thorough search. But now he felt helpless.

A day passed. Then another and then others followed. Lali did not return. My son kept standing in the balcony, looking at the road with unblinking, expectant eyes.

'What was that big problem they were causing you?' My husband asked, an undertone of accusation in his voice. 'As far as I know they never interfered in our life. They stayed in the garage and survived with the leftover food. You had always been intolerant to them. The poor animals got so frightened of you that they ran away from here. Sometimes I doubt it was you who had thrown hot gruel over that puppy!' He said through pursed lips without looking at me.

'Do you believe I could be that cruel?' I snapped back at him. 'Aren't you?' a voice from within charged me. I did not stretch the matter any further.

My son had drawn a picture of a puppy on a piece of paper and captioned it 'Blackie'. He placed the picture on his study table and spent long, quiet hours looking at it. He had stopped inquring about Lali and Blackie. Raghu had in the meantime returned from his village. He searched for the dogs in the neighbourhood but there was no sign of Lali anywhere.

I enacted my role of the ignorant mother quite convincingly. Days rolled on.

One morning my son woke up with a high fever. The temperature measured 105 degree F. we rushed him to the hospital and got him admitted. The treatment started immediately but he did not respond to the treatment. The doctor was worried. 'His reports are all normal. I wonder why the medicine is not working.' He said a little uncertainly. My son was delirious and kept rambling on. One word, 'Blackie' was distinctly audible amidst the incoherent babbles.

'Who is Blackie?" the doctor asked.

'It is a puppy of a native breed. It stayed with us. My son was very fond of it. The puppy has gone away somewhere since two weeks. We have looked everywhere in the neighbourhood but could not find it. My son is missing it badly.'

There was a thoughtful look in the doctor's eyes.

'I think he suffers from an emotional shock, an anxiety syndrome. He was emotionally attached to that puppy. I think you should consult Dr. Mohapatra, the neuro -psychiatrist.

Something inside me splintered into tiny pieces.

'My son needs to be treated by a neuro psychiatrist!'

I was shattered. It was I who was responsible for putting him in this condition. I cursed myself but I could not gather the moral courage to speak out the truth.

We consulted Dr. Mohapatra.

'He had relapsed into a state of major depression. Such a condition ordinarily continues for two weeks or so. But in certain cases it turns to another psychic condition called dysthymia, which is a milder but persistent depression. It is a low mood occurring for at least two years along with some other symptoms of depression. Such a psychic condition is caused by a serious shock the mind experiences when there is a mishap in the house or something of the sort. He will have to remain under treatment and medication at least for a couple of years. I would suggest you get another puppy of similar type for him. It will help him recover early. As we all know the role of the family members is very important in such cases. It is the love and care of one's own people that draws faster response than medicines. It all depends upon you now. The better care you take of him the sooner he will get back to normal. My husband looked at me with gloomy eyes. Something like tear gleamed in the eyes of Raghu.

How helplessly poor Blackie had whimpered inside the gunny sack the gardener had pushed it into!! The muffled whimpering rang in my ears as a constant reminder of my sin.

What was it that Lali's doleful eyes held in that day? Accusation? A silent cursing?

My conscience perhaps had had a blacker shade than that of Blackie's skin.

I stood rooted, my thoughts paralysed.

●●

Grand Father's Notebook

'Tell me a story, grandfather!'

This happened to be my regular demand whenever I was with him. Grandfather never said no. rather he would pick out one after another tales from an inexhaustible reservoir inside him. His eyes shone like the sun, or like the flame of the clay-lamp in the worship-room whenever he narrated a story. Amazed, I stared at that unusual glint in his eyes. I had seen a number of times an involuntary tear trickling down his eyes. But he quickly wiped it off and tried to look easy and normal.

'But these are not stories. They are about the real things that happened in your own life,' I complained, not satisfied. My adolescent mind perhaps wanted something more fanciful, more exciting.

'A story is born at every bend of life's journey,' Grandpa would remark a little absently.

'Really?'

'Yes. What is this life of ours other than a story?' He would try to explain.

I did not make out much of it when he said difficult things like that. But the look in his eyes , his voice suffused with some deep emotion had often distracted me. A disturbing curiosity and a strange sadness that could be defined words had germinated in me even at that tender age. I was as if caught in the euphoria of grandfather's stories and never wanted to come out of that confounding maze. They made me restless, distanced me from my dolls and playmates the common and most appropriate companions of someone at my age. There were stories, may be grandpa's own life events told like a story, which had so overwhelmed me that I could not help asking him who had written it. Grandfather often evaded such a query. 'This is a novel, not a story.' he would say evasively.

'What is a novel?' I would ask unable to hold back my interest.

'Were these novels published in my name!!' he intoned wishfully. At that tender age I had no idea what a novel was. But I guessed that it must be much a longer version of a story.

My incapacity to understand escaped me as a silly smile.

'Can you really write a story?' I asked in an effort to hide the embarrassment of not knowing what a novel was. Grandfather did not answer. He kept looking at some invisible point far off, his face a blank mask. I waited for him to speak. But he remained silent.

I would not know how long grandfather would sit like that, his face expressionless, an absent look in his dull eyes. An hour? Two hours? I got bored and went away to play if it was afternoon, to take a nap if it was noon, or to the tuition class slinging my book-satchel over my shoulder. But when I returned to him after a midday snooze, or from the playground, or from the tuition class he looked the same way. The same distant look lingered in his eyes and a cloud of gloom hung over his face as if he had lost something precious forever. I shrank away from that deep sorrow in his eyes. 'Are you cross with me, grandpa?', I asked guardedly. 'I am not at all sad because you could not write stories. You tell me every day a new story. You have such a huge store house of stories inside you!! I have told all my friends how good a storyteller you are!'

Grandfather looked at me fondly, his face lit up with a childlike guileless smile.

'I know it is only you who will step into the battleground one day laced with the weapon of all my unfulfilled wishes,' he said affectionately.

'What does that mean?'

Grandfather's lips curved in a rueful smile

'I know my child', he said, 'You will be a writer when you grow up. You will write much better stories and novels than me. But you must get your works published in your own name!' I just stared at grandfather, without understanding much.   But I knew instinctively that grandfather wrote not just prayer-verses but stories and novels too. My grandmother too told me stories but she had a limited resource and kept repeating the fairy and the folktales. I got fed up with listening to the same stories again and again. 'I have heard these tales several times. Why don't you tell me new stories?' I demanded. 'I do not know any new story,' grandmother would say conciliatorily. 'I am an unlettered woman. I can tell you only the stories I knew. I am not a poet or a writer like your grandfather. I can't concoct stories out of my imagination like him.'

I discovered the small notebook more by chance than through effort. It lay abandoned, covered in dust in one corner of a bookshelf in the room at the far end of the corridor. The cover page was torn and the pages inside too had gone brittle and yellow. I could recognize the handwriting. It was my grandfather's. It looked like a small account book. Something that looked like a list was written on the pages. There were serial numbers and against every number the title of a book was written. Next to the title there was written a name. Years of neglect had turned the writing on the pages indistinct and faded. I tried to spell out the names of a few books with much effort and searched for them in other bookshelves. But there was no book in our house bearing the titles mentioned in the notebook. The notebook was as confounding as a jigsaw puzzle where not a single piece seemed to fall into place. There was no one reliable whom I could have asked to help me solve the puzzle. It was only grandfather who could have the right answers to the riddle. But grandfather had had a nasty fall in the bathroom and was bedridden. He had suffered a spinal injury which kept him confined to the bed. He lay in his bed, partially paralyzed and showed no sign of any improvement despite all possible treatments. I did not have the heart to ask him about the notebook when he was in such a miserable plight. Mother had never had any interest in literature. Grandmother had never read a book. There was no point in asking either of them about the mysterious notebook. The only alternatives were my father or his sister, my elder aunt. I had heard that my elder aunt was a bright student and she was a connoisseur of books. She had had a fine collection of books in many languages like English, Bengali and Odia. She preserved the books with much care in glass cases like they do in a library. Every book had a serial number. She would dust the books regularly, check the serial numbers and keep them back in neatly arranged stacks. Sometimes my father helped her in cleaning the bookcases and dusting the books.

I could have asked her about the notebook. But there was something in her serious eyes that always made me shrink away from communicating with her. She would punish me at the slightest mistake I made while doing my studies. The stern voice with which she asked me questions sent such a ripple of fear through me that I pissed in my pant. She too, told me stories at times. But she had an altogether different way of doing that. At the end of every story she would ask me a question, 'Tell me what did you learn from this story.' It was like this that I hardly listened to her stories. I just kept nodding my head while my thoughts wandered about aimlessly. I would be thinking if the guava I had identified yesterday in the tree would be ripe by tomorrow, or if my friend Rinki would at all return the eraser she had borrowed from me, or whether or not father would remember to get the children's magazines for me when he came home in the weekend. There were times when I had not heard a sentence of what she said. How could one tell what was the moral of a story without having heard it? I went pale when aunt demanded to tell her what I learnt from the story. She would pinch hard at my thigh. 'Be attentive next time..or else…!!' The hard glare in her eyes explained the rest ….

How desperately I prayed god to make elder aunt to go back to the hostel to continue her studies, or to marry and live in a far off city like Mumbai or Delhi with her family!! If at all I could muster enough courage toask her about the notebook she would charge me of poking my nose into matters that did not concern me and beat me hard. 'What is the need for you to rummage through these old, discarded books and papers?' She would rather charge me than providing any cue to find out a solution and order me to work out arithmetic sums, write an essay or to do translation.

There were still four days before father came home

on his weekly visit. And even then too it was not easy to find him alone for asking about grandfather's mysterious notebook. As soon as he arrived in the evening of Saturday he would get engaged in taking care of a number of domestic details. He would inquire if grandfather had been taking his medicines regularly and was there any noticeable improvement in his condition. He would inspect the progress in the construction of the new house and pay the masons and the labourers their weekly wage, and many such things that had waited weeklong to be attended to. The list would go on and on. I decided that I would better ask father about the notebook on Sunday morning after coming back from the tuition class. At that hour, I hoped, he would be alone. I hid the notebook where no one could notice it and went to sleep. But, father kept busy all through theday. I was desperately looking for an opportunity to find him alone and tried to be around him on different pretexts. It was almost evening when he finally called me to him. 'I know why are you so restless', he said stroking my head affectionately. 'You are eager to know if I brought your magazines. Aren't you? I am sorry. I could not bring them this time. But I promise I will surely get them in the next weekend.' I had nothing to say to that. Father left for his workplace and I had to hold my curiosity back with all the effort I could use. But I was careful enough not to let the notebook fall into anyone else's hand. Time and again I would go to the room at the far end of the veranda making different excuses to ascertain that the notebook was there in its place. 'What are you doing there in that room?' A loud voice startled me as I was checking one evening if the notebook was there or not. It was my grandmother. 'I was looking for a book', I said lamely. 'Why don't you turn on the light, then? What book are you searching in the dark?' She demanded. I came out of the room and without answering left the place closing the door gently behind me.

That night, after dinner, I went to grandfather's room. A small zero power bulb scattered a feeble light around. Grandfather lay asleep. I did not have the heart to disturb him. I stood by the door and looked, my eyes wet. He had gone through a hell lot of pain during last few days. I had seen how his face creased in pain when the injection syringe was pushed into his spinal cord. He did not let a word of complaint escape him when he was made to swallow the bitter pills, or the Ayurvedic therapist of *Kalupada Ghat* pressed the red hot poker on his knees and waist I could almost feel the singe on my body. My eyes blinded with tears I blundered out to the verandah. 'What a diabolical sinner the man is!' I thought partly with pity and partly with fear. 'Didn't he have even a grain of pity in his heart?" Mother said that the therapy would cure grandfather and he would get back to his normal shape soon. But something deep inside me told me not to believe her. The thing that made me more sad than the pressing of that burning hot poker on grandfather's waist and knees was the look in my grandfather's eyes. It was a blend of sheer despair and anguish. One moment in that pair of dull eyes there blazed a cruel flame of pain and suffering that charred his helpless despondency to a pile of black ash in the next. I could almost translate that look into words...

'This is the end. I will never be normal again,' it said. 'I cannot bear this terrible pain any longer.' But he never said any of these.

Why didn't grandfather ever make a complaint or let out a scream of anger? Why did not he yell out his protest as I used to do while mother made me swallow that evil smelling liquid when I had had a fever? Why did not he howl as I did when I was given an injection? Why did he keep quiet and just looked at nothing with a pair of unblinking, cloudy eyes? I could not fathom the mystery of it. These days I could not bring myself to ask grandfather to tell a story. I shied away from that strange, indecipherable look in his eyes. I remembered noticing a similar sort of dispassion and emptiness in his eyes whenever he told me a story even when he was perfectly well. But that blank detachment in his eyes had multiplied several times after he got confined to the bed. I could understand that the suffering he was passing through had brought that empty look into his eyes. But what made his eyes so dull and miserable when he was in sound health? What pain in what part of his body made him look like that? I failed to figure it out. And what was that mysterious notebook that looked like an accounts book? What sort of account was recorded there? The curiosity raised its obstinate head again in me defeating all my conscientious argument that grandfather was not in a condition to be disturbed for such little things.

The opportunity came soon. My elder aunt was not at home that day. Grandmother and mother were in the outer courtyard examining the strange and rare products Ukii showed them. Ukii lived in the snake charmers' colony in the suburbs. She came at intervals carrying interesting and out-of-our reach objects like the tooth of an elephant, the whiskers of a tiger, and many such things in her basket. She would put down her basket in our outer courtyard and call out loudly for my grandmother and mother. Mother used to give her a large bowl of watered rice. She also gave her our cast off dresses for her children. Both mother and grandmother would then sit looking with interest at the strange things in Ukii's basket. Sometimes they bought a thing or two from her too. I knew that once Ukii came she would not leave at least for an hour or so.

Finding my long awaited chance I tiptoed into grandfather's room. Grandfather was awake. I walked up to him. He stopped me as I was about to sit down by his side on his bed. 'Do not sit on this bed my child', he said. 'You might catch an infection. Don't you see I am wallowing in my own excretions? Sit in that chair'. He pointed at the straight-backed chair that stood by the bed. But I ignored his warning and sat close to him. Without giving him time to say anything more I took out the notebook and held it before him. Grandfather raised his head from the pillow a little and craning his neck peered at the notebook. 'What is it?' He asked. 'That is what I have come to ask *you*,' I said. 'What kind of an account book is this?' I brought the notebook a little closer to his eyes. Even then he could not see it clearly. ' I can't see clearly. Will you read it out for me?' 'It is in your writing,' I said. I cannot make anything out of it. I found this in the room at the far end corner of the veranda. It was lying by your old trunk , the one you had while you worked in Calcutta. It looks like a list or something. There are serial numbers. Against each serial number there is written the title of a story or a book and there was a name against each such title there is the name of someone…''Oh, that notepad!!' Grandfather broke in. It is an old notepad. I had jotted down the names of a few books there. There would be thirty three such titles there. Actually there should have been thirty five titles, or thirty six. I can't remember correctly now. I had not added the rest two or three titles.' Grandfather sounded animated and effusive. I gaped at him, unable to understand a thing. 'But what have you serialized them in this way for? The thirty five or thirty six names you have jotted down in this notepad,' I asked curiously,' What are those?' Grandfather stopped short. The effusiveness had gone from his voice. He closed his eyes. 'It was nothing important. You are not old enough to understand these things. Now be a good girl and go away. I want to sleep.' He turned his face away.

For the first time in my life I was cross with my grandfather that day. I might not have fathomed the mystery shrouding the thin and small notepad. But I could guess that he was holding something back. What was it grandfather wanted to hide from me? What was the secret the wrinkled sepia pages of the small notebook held? I came out of the room consumed by an overwhelming curiosity.

From that moment onwards a strange restlessness took hold of me. My thoughts hovered constantly around the small old notepad which, by now I had guessed, held some secret which grandfather did not want to share with me.

The class annual examination was drawing near, but I could not concentrate in my studies. I had not had the nerve to ask father about the notebook after grandfather revealed his reluctance to discuss it. And quite surprisingly, since the day I had asked him about the notepad, grandfather had never mentioned it, not even once. The obviousness with which he had tried to elude the subject made me even more infuriated. Goaded by a passion that was a blend of curiosity and suspiciousness I kept on looking for something that would give me a clue to solve the mystery of the notebook. I opened the trunk in which grandfather kept his personal effects while he worked with the Railway Mail Service at Calcutta. There were two pairs of old Railway Uniform, a pair of coat and pants, a few copies of prayer-songs which grandfather had written, some old official documents relating to the farm lands in the trunk. There was nothing to catch my notice except for bulky handwritten copybook. The handwriting was grandfather's, sloppy and clumsy. There was no caption on the cover page. Feeling excited at this unexpected discovery I turned over the cover and found something written in the next page.

'I dedicate this dossier that details the account of all the sin and virtues of my entire life to Mother Goddess Sarala who had showered her blessings on an ignorant fellow like me and prompted me on to write. I also dedicate this to my granddaughter who carries a whole new world of artistic creativity within her.....'

In the next page there was something that was more or less like a testimony. It explained what made him write that novel. And the novel proper began in the following page under a heading that said Part One. Overwhelmed with an indescribable joy at this eureka moment I rushed to grandfather's room. All my grievances and complaints against him had vanished into thin air. I was breathless from running hard and from the excitement at the discovery when I entered his room. A strange stench hung in the air. Perhaps grandfather had urinated in the bed. By this time his left side was paralyzed. Ignoring the smell I ran to his bed and shook him by his shoulder ..

'Grandfather, ' I almost yelled, ' Isn't this your handwriting? I know this is your writing. Is this a novel you haver written? Could it be printed in your name? Can I show this to my friends and tell them that my grandfather has written it?' I shot a series of questions at him without waiting for him to say anything. He lay all soaked in his urine. A drop of tear trickled down his half-closed eye.

'Go and ask your mother to clean up this mess and change the bedspread. I have been calling out for someone to help but it seems no one is around anywhere near.' He saidwithout answering a single one of my questions.

The surging rush of euphoria in me ebbed abruptly. I went outside and called my mother to attend to grandfather. After she came into the room and started cleaning the bed I went to the roof top carrying the bulky copy with me. I thought no one would disturb me there. I opened the copy and tried to read but could not go beyond two pages. Grandfather's writing was clumsy and not very legible. The first two pages narrated the growth of a family tree. The first man at the root of the tree was a total stranger to me. The torture his step mother inflicted on him forced him to leave his native place (it was either Calcutta or Bhagalpur) for good and settled at a place which over the years became the village we came to know as our own. His progenies established themselves in that village. My grandfather arrived in the picture after five or six such generations. They were three brothers and sisters. Grandfather's parents succumbed to some epidemic when his elder sister was a child-widow of nine. Grandfather was seven and his younger brother was four. All their properties were usurped by their relatives through deceit driving the three orphaned kids practically to the road. The nine year old sister had to face a lot of hardship to take care of her brothers. After a year or so my grandfather went away to Calcutta in search of a job. He was engaged as a houseboy in a Bengali family and settled there. He resumed his studies too. In the meanwhile the cruel indifference of the villagers and abject poverty forced his sister to kill herself. After her death my grandfather returned to Calcutta with his younger brother. Thereafter began my grandfather's fierce struggle for survival, his crusade against destiny. 'Come down and say your evening prayers', mother called out for me as I was about to move on to the next page and I had to come down holding my raging curiosity in check with a great effort. I kept back the copy in that last room at the far end corner of the verandah and came to the worship-room. After the evening worship I went to look at grandfather. He was sleeping. I returned. During that evening I went to look at grandfather a number of times goaded by a desire to draw out the secret from him, and to decipher the coded look in his eyes. I stood by the door and peeped inside. Every time I found grandfather sleeping in the same posture. He lay still and there was almost no movement in his body. his face was partly hidden by a thick growth of beard. On Sunday morning father would get the barber to shave it clean. Every Sunday father would call the barber to shave grandfather's beard. He would lift grandfather in his arms and took him to the courtyard, bathe him, wipe him dry and then sit him in an easy chair. He would put long pillows behind him to give support to his back. After grandfather settled comfortably father would talk to him. He would tell him about the farming and harvesting and the annual yielding of the crops. Then he would feed grandfather rice and prawn curry coaxing him to have more helpings of the prawn curry, But grandfather would refuse to eat more saying that he could not digest it. 'Tell me what would you like to eat. I will get it from Cuttack,' father would ask fondly.' 'My days are numbered', grandfather would reply dryly. 'I have no wish left for good food'.

' Why do you say such things? The doctor assures that you will be all right. It will just take a little time. This is not paralysis. Only a nerve has been damaged. But the injections and vitamins will soon heal it.' Father would sound very convincing while saying it.

All this time I would be sitting on the verandah

swinging my legs, watching father and grandfather and listening to their conversation.

I had heard the doctor saying to my father that grandfather would never be normal again. Why did then father lie to him? Why did grandfather say that he would not live for long? Who would tell me stories if he died? Who would tell me about the notebook and the handwritten manuscript of the novel? Who would answer the questions that haunted me day and night? And, the most important of them all, whom shall I call grandfather if he died? Something like a red hot lump got stuck at my throat.

After grandfather had eaten his midday meal father would carry him back to his room and put him in the bed. 'Grandfather will remain imprisoned inside the four walls of his room till next Sunday,' I thought gloomily, 'cut off from the outside world.'

Grandfather began lapsing into a delirious state of mind and ramble on disjointed subjects. He lost the sense of time and suffered some kind of a memory-confusion. *'Nani, Nani...* He would call out loudly his sister who had died years ago. He could not know if the clothes he wore were in place or had slipped off his body. Sometimes he would keep on singing a prayer loudly until someone stopped him. Grandmother said that he was getting disoriented. a sharp pain like a knife stab tore at my heart as I watched the progressive deterioration of his health. Despite all the disinfectants used to keep the room fresh and tidy the musty smell of decay lingered obstinately in its air. And grandfather was slowly and steadily wearing away inside those four walls.

It was the auspicious day of *Saraswati Puja*(Saraswati, the goddess of art and wisdom was worshipped on this day). I wore my new dress and went to grandfather's room to get his blessings. He signaled me to come closer to him. 'There is a bulky copybook in my old trunk.' He said, stammering. 'Get it'.

'What is written in that copybook?' the words escaped me before I could stop them.

'It is a testimony,' he said.

'What is a testimony?'

'It is the story of my life,' he said unsteadily, 'Get it.'

'And, the small notebook with the torn cover,' I broke in. 'What is it? Shall I bring that too?'

' Just do what much I ask you,' grandfather sounded impatient.

I ran to the lone room at the end of the verandah and brought out the thick copybook from the trunk and gave it to grandfather. He ran his hand gently on it, like he was caressing someone he loved a lot.

'I have spent many sleepless nights to write it,' he reminisced. 'I had scribbled on while travelling in train. I wrote sitting on the roadside. I wrote sitting on a bench outside a courtroom. There were times when I woke up in the middle of the night and scribbled on afraid I might forget something if I waited for the morning. This is the testament of all the struggle and hardship of my life. Go through it and preserve it carefully. You will get the answers of all your questions here. I know you will have trouble in reading my handwriting. I thought I would read out the passages and you would take them down in your handwriting. We would then get it printed and send it to a publisher. It will be my first published book. Why first.. it would rather be my thirty sixth book....!!' grandfather stopped abruptly as if he had committed some sort of a crime and said something which he should not have said.

'But this misfortune befell me out of nowhere,' he said changing the topic. 'I will not be able to read out even a page to you in my present condition. You see how I stammer while speaking. Tears are continuously trickling down my eyes making it impossible for me to read even a few lines. One side of my body has gone paraplegic. Your father is hiding the truth from me, but I know everything. I am not a kid. I would hold no grievance against my destiny if this one book at least got published in my name. You will have to read it yourself or ask your father (he could read my handwriting) to read it out for you. You copy it down neatly and get it printed. I have not decided a title for the book. You have to think of one that sounds appropriate to you.' Grandfather stopped talking and closed his eyes.

My thoughts were caught up in a wild whirl as I listened to him. I find it so difficult to describe the shocking impact grandfather's words made on me that morning. (It still lives fresh in me. I feel a constriction at my throat, my body goes numb, I get soaked all over with perspiration and copious tears run down my eyes every time the moment came back to me.)

I remember I was blinded by tears as I stood there, overwhelmed with sorrow and surprise, listening to him. ' I will surely get it published, grandfather,' I promised in a voice choked with tears. 'And it will be published in *your* name.' His face lit up. He opened his eyes and smiled at me. There was the same glow in his eyes which I often noticed whenever he told me a story.

'I know you will carry my name forward. I trust you kid. That is why I am asking you to fulfill this last wish of mine and leave my most precious possession in your custody.' I gripped his right palm looking straight into his wet, expectant eyes 'Yes, yes,' I promised again. 'I will fulfill all your wishes. Would you now tell me what is there in that small notepad?'

Forget the notepad. I feel so relieved. I can now die in peace.' He said and closed his eyes again.

I do not remember now how long I kept standing there, as if I was under some kind of a spell. I regained my composure when the gentle snoring of grandfather reached my ears. I went to my study room and put the copy carefully in a folder. I kept the folder in my book-shelf. A few days after the whole body of grandfather became paralyzed. He lost his speech too. There was no movement in his body. The only sign of life left in him was the flicker in his eyes. He was now fed with liquids only. It was getting unbearable for me to see grandfather in such a pathetic condition. I could not share my feelings with anyone but something was eating my liveliness away.

The loud wailing of my grandmother and mother jolted me out of sleep that morning. I ran down the staircase, two steps at a time. A crowd had gathered in the courtyard. Mother and grandmother were crying miserably. Father sat on the veranda leaning against the wall, looking dejected and broken. 'Your grandfather has left us!' Mother blurted amidst choking sobs.

How did I receive that truth? How did I react to it? Did I cry? Was I shocked to a frozen silence? I can't recollect it correctly now. It was all a blurred, hazy memory of an indefinable experience.

It was a fortnight or so after grandfather's death. The funeral rituals were over. Father sat in the courtyard in an armchair, his face clouded, looking vaguely up at the sky. I walked up to him and sat beside him.

'Grandfather had given me a copybook,' I said breaking the gloomy silence.

'What copybook?' father looked questioningly at me.
'It is the manuscript of a novel. He said it was the story of his own life!'

Father sprang up from the chair. 'When did he do that? Why haven't you told me about it? Is the copy book with you? Show it to me.' He sounded so anxious that I ran to my study room and rushed back to him, carrying the plastic folder. I brought the small notebook too. I handed the folder to him.

' He had asked me to keep it. I tried to read but it was not easy. The letters were so small!!' I explained apologetically.

'I can read his handwriting,' father said. 'I am familiar with his writing since I was a child. I will read it out to you and you can get them copied in your neat hand in another notebook. We will get it printed and then send it to a publisher.'

'There is this small notepad, too, I Said and gave him the small notebook. 'There was a list of some books or something in it. But I could not make anything out of that list, nor did grandfather tell me anything when I asked him about it.' father took the notepad and looked at it closely. He put on his glasses and turned the pages and read for some time.

'This is the list of the books he had written,' father said trying to hold the teardrops that hung precariously at the corner of his eyes in check.

'And the books? What happened to them?' I asked.

'He had not published those in his own name. He had sold the manuscripts to people who got them published in their individual names and earned the publicity of a writer. Some books were written in Odia and some were written in Bengali. There were even some which were adapted into plays and were enacted. But father had never disclosed the names of the people who had bought his manuscripts.'

'But why did grandfather do such a thing?' I asked, too surprised to guess a thing.

'Poverty!!' Father replied wetly. 'Abject poverty had forced him to do that. We were just kids then. He had to run the household and at the same time fight a lawsuit in the court to get back his own ancestral lands from the illegal possession of his kinsmen. His meagre earning was not enough to meet all these expenses. So he sold the books which he wrote with so much passion.'

'How do you know all this?'

'I have seen how hard he struggled to make both ends meet. He wrote books keeping awake through the nights. But he had never published them. Nor had he ever mentioned a manuscript once he had sold it to someone.'

Several times thereafter I had ran a loving hand over the notebook, turned it up and down on my palms and squinted at it through my vaporous tears, overwhelmed with a terrible remorse.

My school finals were round the corner. I went to the school hostel a few days before the examination to do my studies in a purely academic environment. Fearing that that I might misplace the copy in the hostel I left it at home. I had decided that I would copy the entire manuscript down with the help of my father during the summer holidays. While I was in the hostel my mother fell ill and was admitted in the hospital. She had to undergo a surgery and so she remained in the hospital for some days.

I came back home after the examination was over. To my dismay I did not find grandfather's copybook at the place where I had kept it. I frantically searched the missing manuscript at all possible places in the house. But the book was nowhere in the house. Thoroughly disheartened I asked mother if she had seen the copybook anywhere.

'Ask your aunt. I had left the house in her charge while I was in the hospital. She might have sold it away along with all other old books and papers to the man who bought old newspapers and scraps.'

It felt as if the sky had come crashing down on me. An icy wave of utter loss swept over me numbing my senses.

'You have taken away all the books and copies that were important to you to the hostel. There were stacks of useless old books and papers in that room. They just gathered dust lying there. Who would have needed to read them? I sold them to the man who collected old papers and magazines in order to clean the room. There was perhaps a bulky copybook of your grandfather was among the lot. I now remember seeing it. The writing was so illegible I could not read a word. Of what use it would have been?'

●●

The Brahma Demon

The Polmunda chowk came just after the jackfruit orchard that stretched beyond the Maquddam chowk. After about a distance of two or three hundred meters along a track that led off the Polmunda chowk towards the left, there stood a gigantic Banyan tree by the roadside. The Brahma-Demon, the spirit of the Brahmin Luna Panda, who had died young, settled there. The demon is said to have made that tree its abode for the last fifteen years or so. There are supposed to be different categories in the ghost community, too. But topping the hierarchy is the Brahma-Demon, who, it is said, possesses great supernatural power. A Brahmin, who dies young, with many of his wishes gone unfulfilled, would become a Brahma-demon. It can create unusual trouble in the world of the living if it willed so.

The ghost of Luna Panda is believed to have been living in that huge tree for the last fifteen years. But time has not mellowed its aggressiveness. Anyone who passed by the road after nine in the night, was bound to feel its presence. He might hear uncanny sounds like a big bird suddenly taking to flight flapping its wings, or the rattle of a branch breaking. Sometimes the silence would be filled with the eerie splashes of dried up cakes of earth falling in a scatter or the thwacks of stones thrown from invisible sources. Sometimes one could have a vision, which might be more an imagination than actuality, of something like a shapeless shadow hanging from the branches. That was how the Brahma-demon made his presence felt to the passersby.

To the young men of the modern age with an empirical mind, such tales may seem absurd and baseless. But listening to such things time and again from their elders, too, had shaken their scientifically oriented convictions a little.

The eighty year or more than that old grandmother in the Pradhan family happened to have the first hand knowledge of how Luna Panda had died. It was she who had given an oil massage to Luna Panda while he was an infant, and it was she who had witnessed his cremation, a morbid, bizarre affair!! There were only three others, who were there with her. Those three were the major characters in the strange story. The episode of Luna Panda could begin with these three, Daiya, his wife Sushi and Sushi's elder daughter Nandini. These are the major characters in the 'Luna Panda' story.

It was a late afternoon of early winter. The sun was about to go down the western skyline. The twilight was a mysterious blend of the fast fading daylight and the transparent black of the approaching evening. Daiya pedaled his bicycle towards the outer courtyard of his house. It was routine work for him to carry vegetables to the village marketplace to sell them at a better price. It was usually late evening by the time he returned home from the market place. But, business was good on that day and all his vegetables were sold away quickly.

Just as he got off the bicycle, Sushi, his wife, came out of the house rolling her disheveled hair to a knot at the back of her head. In that quasi darkness their eyes met for a fraction of a moment and Sushi walked away saying that she was going out to the field to relieve herself. Daiya stepped on to the verandah. He was about to toss his *gamchha* up at the thatch but stopped abruptly as the sound of a muffled coughing of a man. The sound came from inside the house. 'Who is that?' Daiya yelled and rushed into the house. It was not possible to see anything clearly in the dark but his feet touched something like a human body and as Daiya pounced upon it, a pair of hands grabbed at his feet. 'It is me Daiya bhai!' a voice whimpered from the dark. 'Who? Luna Babu?' Daiya, shocked out of wit, released the man. What else could he have done? There were other options, though. He could have screamed at the top of his voice, called at the neighbours , or had kicked at or showered blows on Luna Panda. But he did nothing of the sort. Instead, he strode out of the room, slumped on the outer verandah and gazed blankly at the stars that were beginning to peep out.

Luna Panda brought goat meat that night to Daiya's house and cooked the meat himself. As they sat eating the meat cooked in delicious gravy, Luna Panda pampered him to eat more than he should have eaten. 'Have some more of it Daiya bhai!' He kept on coaxing. Daiya would have liked to ponder over some obvious questions that haunted him, like what were Luna Panda and his wife Sushi doing in the darkness of that room in Daiya's absence? But he drove the disturbing thoughts away from his mind. He did not even curse his wife or called her a whore having it off with another man.

Sushi, however, wore a guilty look on her face for a few days. But life soon returned to normal and both Daiya and Sushi accepted each other as if nothing had happened. Luna Panda kept on frequenting their house.

The legacy of servility that had been passed on

from his parents to Daiya had always bridled the storming passion that hit at his male- pride.

In fact the homestead actually was Luna Panda's property. The house, where Daiya and his wife lived, lawfully belonged to Luna Panda. Daiya knew that his parents had lived on the charity of the Panda family. His father worked as a farmhand, looked after the cows in the cowshed. His mother looked after almost all the household affairs including the cooking. Luna was the eighteenth child of his parents. All the seventeen children born before him had not survived. A pregnancy a year and the delivering of eighteen children had accelerated the aging process in Luna's mother and rendered her incapable of any work that demanded physical labour. It was Daiya's mother who took care of her and catered to all her needs. Sashi Ma, Luna's mother had never looked down upon Daiya and treated her differently from her own son. Although the family of Daiya had served Luna Panda's family for years and years, the master –servant relationship had never affected the genuine liking the families had for each other.

Daiya's father died rather prematurely. He was bitten by a poisonous snake while he was working in the paddy field. Shortly after, Daiya's mother, who had gone into a shock, followed her husband to the other world. Daiya was only fifteen or so at that time. Luna was just a few years younger. His father had died years before. As long as Daiya's parents lived they used to take care of Sashi Ma, Luna's mother. After their death Sashi Ma became Daiya's sole responsibility. The old woman had developed a bad sprain in her left ankle and she was not able to walk. Her hands were trembling and she was not able to keep a grip over the things she held. She had pleaded that Daiya should move in with them to their house and accordingly Daiya came to live in an isolated corner in the Panda house. Daiya had to cook, look after the household affairs and take care of the ailing woman. The lands, however, were given away for croft farming. While Daiya, at that tender age, sagged under the heterogeneity of the responsibilities stacked on his shoulder, Luna Panda was preparing for his matriculation examination. It was only a pretext though, because while he was supposed to be studying, he actually was poring over the pages that contained nude and obscene pictures of girls. The unlettered Daiya often wondered if questions in the matriculation examination came from such horrible books.

Luna Panda sat for the examination not once but five times, year after year, but could not get through it successfully. Sashi Ma had lost all hopes on her son. She insisted that Daiya must marry and bring a bride who, she said, would share his responsibility. Daiya married and Sushi, who had read up to class seven, came as a bride to his house. Life became a lot easier after Sushi came. She took full charge of the household, much in the same way , Daiya's mother did, and Daiya began to turn his attention to farming. Sashi Ma, Luna Panda's mother, in the mean while, had become totally immobile and remained confined to the bed. Sushi and Daiya took full care of her including the cleaning of her wastes. She did not live long however, and passed quietly away in one night. Luna Panda was not at home. Nor was there any news of him or his whereabouts. After a long wait, it was decided by the village people that Daiya would ignite to the pyre of the old lady. Luna Panda returned on the fourth day of his mother's death, stayed till the last rites for the departed soul were observed and went away again. He used to stay away from home for days on end, returned for a few days and again went back. Nobody knew where did he go or what he did when he was not home.

Luna's mother had made the wish that the family of Daiya would continue to own the homestead plot at the back of Luna's house. 'Daiya had been working in our family since he was a young boy. You must let his family live there permanently. They would build their house and stay on.' Luna Panda had not acted against his mother's wish. So, Daiya and his wife continued to live in the Panda house even after the death of Luna's mother. And Luna Panda continued to make the brief visits to the house at short and long intervals as it suited to his mood and his wish.

Sushi opened the lock of Luna's room, cleaned and dusted and put a pitcher of water in one corner. She collected the dirty clothes and washed them. She cooked Luna Panda's favourite dishes in those days when Luna Panda stayed with them. It did not often catch Daiya's notice since his mind was preoccupied with the farming, tending of the cows and milking them and the problems involved therein, but Sushi seemed to take good care of her own looks when Luna Panda was there in the house. She had her hair neatly done in a braid. She wore a clean sari and applied some cosmetics to her face. Sushi was a beautiful woman, slightly dusky, but had sharp, chiseled features like those of some goddess. It had never entered Daiya's mind that there could be a special reason for Sushi to deck herself. He neither had time nor the courage to ask Luna Panda where he had been all these days. Nor could he say to him that it was high time Luna Panda got married, looked after his own lands and the farming and let Daiya live his own uncomplicated life.

Every time Luna Panda left after his brief stay at the house, he shoved some good money into Daiya's hand and stored ration for Daiya's family that would last months. All this favour had sealed Daiya's lips.

Time and again the elderly people of the village tried to open his eyes to reality. Though they did not mention it openly but made well concealed remarks on the possibility of Luna Panda's illegitimate relation with his wife. But Daiya glared at them whenever they tried to broach the topic and that stopped them. 'The lucky devil!', some used to say when Daiya was not listening. 'The son of a milkman, the fellow is living the life of a rich Brahmin.' 'It was all because of his wife,' someone else remarked. 'It was she who has changed his fate.'

After a few years Sushi gave birth to a beautiful baby girl. The rumor that Luna Panda was the baby's real father, spread fast in the village. In fact, the baby girl seemed to have taken after Luna Panda. She was fair complexioned and extremely lovely. Was the baby actually his own child? Daiya was not feeling very sure. He was dark, and Sushi too was not fair. Where did the baby get that bright complexion? They had not had a baby till Luna Panda appeared on the scene. His mind was in a terrible whirr. Perhaps the long standing obligation to the Panda family and the servility that had entered deep into his marrow conquered his better judgment and compelled him to swallow the venom of humiliation.

'Daiya Bhai,' Luna Panda said during one such visit to the village. 'I am going to Bombay. I may or may not return. I am leaving all this property in your charge. It is up to you how you handle it.' he sold away a large part of the landed property and went away with the money.' 'The rest of the property is all yours,' he said before leaving. 'You must take care of your daughter's education and get her married in a good family.' Daiya felt even more obliged; his eyes became wet with tears of gratitude. But Sushi showed no reaction. Luna Panda went away and did not return.

Days turned to months and months became years. People, as it was obvious, made their individual speculations. Some said that he had already died, while others surmised that he was involved in some illegal business and the police had arrested him. There were still some who remarked that he had travelled overseas to another country. Things were changing in Daiya's life too. Sushi was looking older and their school going daughter was growing up fast.

But Luna Panda returned, proving everyone wrong.

The news, however, preceded his return.

It was shocking, unbelievable news. In no time it spread like wildfire through Luna Panda's own village and through its neighbouring ones. The news, a very small item, was published in a daily news paper along with a photo of Luna Panda. It said that a man from that particular village, who lived in Bombay was diagnosed with the dreaded disease AIDS. He was sent to the medical college at Cuttack for treatment but the hospital authority had refused to admit the patient and returned him to his native place. The news, though occupied a short space in the news paper, hit hard at the complacent mindset of the village people. They knew AIDS was incurable and was a killer and a contagious disease. So the news of Luna Panda's return sent a stir of fright through the village.

That day, the press reporters both from print and electronic media flocked into Luna Panda's village and gathered about his house much before the ambulance carrying Luna Panda arrived. They slammed questions at Daiya and his family. 'Why are you living in Luna Panda's house? Are you related to him? How long since he had been suffering from this disease? Have you been excommunicated because of this reason? What a sort of troubles you are facing on account of this?' The questions went on and on, unendingly. Daiya did not say a word, as if he had turned to stone; Sushi wept and whimpered some unintelligible reply. The TV people kept on badgering them in their professional manner but could not extract any stuff out of them which could have made them build up a savoury story for their respective channels. After a long time they rode away in their vans. But the mood of repulsion and loathing they had built up took the entire village in its grip. As soon as the vans left, the people pounced upon Daiya and Sushi.

'It is a highly contagious disease,' they said. 'Sushi must have contracted the dreaded disease from Luna Panda. So too have Daiya and their daughter.' Daiya's family was to be ostracized, they decided unanimously. Their daughter was not allowed entry at the school.

'Didn't I tell you long back that Daiya's wife was having an illegitimate relationship with Luna Panda, and that they should be driven away from our village? And look at Daiya! What innocence he pretends! He has made himself a slave of that whore of his wife.' Someone spat out. 'He is bearing with this humiliation because of his greed for Luna Panda's huge property. No husband would let his wife sleep with another man otherwise!' Another inferred. 'What a shame! What a shame!'

The words did not enter Daiya's ears. He sat woodenly on the verandah, his face a blank mask. Sushi had gone inside the house with her daughter. 'The ambulance carrying Luna Panda is here' a voice said loudly. 'I have heard the driver asking the way to his house,' it added. The crowd that had thronged in front of the house dispersed. People ran back to the safety of their homes. The front yard of Luna Panda's house was deserted almost in no time.

Sushi came out and stood on the verandah. She had not cooked that day. A strange lassitude had settled over her, numbing her body and mind. The sun blazed hard and hunger flamed inside their empty stomachs. Something that was a blend of fear and despair choked her insides. 'Have I contracted it?' the question kept gnawing at her mind.

What must she do now? Sushi felt torn apart. Should she leave the man who had done so much for her to die such a pathetic death? She owed everything to him. The house, the cows, the farmlands, the granary-full crops she and Daiya owned actually and lawfully belonged to Luna Panda. It was Luna Panda who had given her a fulfilled life! a home and a child too! Could she ever deny that? Could she ever loath and repel him as others did and turn him out saying that he was not wanted here, in his own house? Wouldn't it be a sin?

Sushi watched the ambulance as it pulled up in front of the house. The driver was speaking to Daiya. Three men came out carrying Luna Panda. 'Where will we put him?' They asked looking at Sushi. She pointed a finger at the old spring cot on the verandah, 'there', an almost inaudible, wet voice escaped her.

She kept standing motionless in the sun till long after the men had left after slumping Luna Panda on that rickety cot.

'Ma,' her daughter called from the verandah. 'Perhaps uncle wants to say something.' Sushi walked up the steps to the verandah and peered at the man lying on the cot.

A robust, bright complexioned handsome man of more than six feet height was reduced to an ugly frame of skeletons covered in a gnarled, brittle layer of skin. As if all blood has been sucked away from his body! Does approaching death make everyone look this horrid? Almost like a ghost!! Ugly strands of matted, rusty hair straggled about a pale, ghostly face that was covered with unkempt beard. A tear rolled down her eyes!

'He is asking for some water, perhaps,' Sushi's daughter said again.

Sushi swallowed back the deep sigh and got some water in a glass. She sat down on the cot by Luna Panda. She lifted his head carefully and cradling it in the crook of left arm and hand, she tried to make him drink water from the glass she held in the other hand. Luna Panda opened his eyes and looked at Sushi. His sunken eyes held a look of some unspeakable sorrow. He drank a little water with much effort. He tried to say something with a feeble motioning of his hand. 'Come here,' Sushi called her daughter. 'I am holding his head in place. Try to put some water through his lips.' The girl did as told. The next moment Luna Panda's head dropped back in an awkward angle. His eyes closed but the lips remained parted. Sushi did not understand what happened. But her loud scream jolted Daiya back to action and he hurried in to see what had happened.

Luna Panda had died.

The death of Luna Panda was another disaster. Daiya knew that the village people would not touch the dead body. Could he carry the body alone to the cremation ground of the village? Would he burn the body or bury it? Daiya's mind refused to function. An hour passed. Daiya was still not sure what was he going to do with the body. The news of Luna Panda's death travelled fast. Again a large crowd gathered before the house. The *Sarpanch* and other elderly people firmly refused to allow Luna Panda's dead a customary cremation at the village crematory ground.

Sushi came out, the end part of her sari wound tightly around her waist.

'Carry the fire wood from the stack outside the kitchen and keep them in the plantain-orchard at the backyard of the house,' She asked her daughter. 'No need to take his body to the cremation ground,' she declared in a loud voice.' His pyre will be lit in the backyard of his own house! It is his own place and no one in the village has the right to refuse!' Sushi yelled. She wore a disheveled look and there was an odd glitter in her dry eyes. She looked like she was possessed by some spirit.

The body was set on the pyre in the plantain-orchard. People flocked about to watch. Sushi set fire to a log of wood. Holding the log that burnt fiercely she walked up to Daiya. 'Here, 'She said pushing the flaming log into his hand, 'Set fire to the funeral pyre!' Daiya moved like an automaton and torched the pyre. The dry logs began to burn in wild flames.

'Nandini!' Sushi called her eldest daughter. 'Come here. Take this and hold the flame to the face of *your* father.' She shouted over the crackle of the burning wood as she handed another burning log to the young girl. 'Let his soul repose in peace!'

The people gaped at Sushi, stunned, speechless. So was Daiya.

She looked around wildly and before anyone could say anything she ran inside and returned carrying a billhook. 'Be Ware!' She shouted at the crowd waving menacingly the hand that gripped the billhook. 'I will hack the one to pieces that opens his mouth!!' She screamed at the top of her voice.

Daiya, paralyzed with shock at the unexpectedness of what had happened, stared at Sushi.

She looked like a stranger to him.

●●

Festival of Fire

Dama took the *gamchha* off his shoulder and put it down. A bundle made at one of its ends unrolled and four brinjals, and a couple of potatoes spilled out of it. 'This is all mother let me bring here,' he said. 'I have plucked a few brinjals from our vegetable garden,' Gora said. 'There are a few potatoes too,' he added. 'I have brought only potatoes,' Dhruva joined. 'My mother has counted them and warned me to take them all back tomorrow morning.'

It was a full moon night of the fire festival that is celebrated in the last one of the winter months. A huge bonfire was lit at an open space of the village and people flung vegetables into it as the customary offerings to the fire god. In the morning they would collect the roasted vegetables from the piles of ash and take them back home to eat. Dama , Gora and Dhruva stood by the blazing fire. It was Dhruva whose eyes fell on *him* first.

A figure looking like a shapeless shadow limped painfully towards the spot.

'Look at that!!' Dhruva nudged his friends. 'Isn't he the ' Banshi the Lame'?' Gora and Dama turned to look at the figure Dhruva was pointing at. It was the 'Banshi the Lame' all right. His name was Banshi. But he had lost one of his legs in an unfortunate accident and walked wonkily.

He was nicknamed as the 'Banshi the Lame' .The village urchins laughed, clapped and made fun of him whenever he came into sight. Dhruva, Dama and Gora started clapping and singing ...

' Banshi the lame ! Banshi the Lame!
How many coins have you kept
Tucked in the folds of the cloth at your waist!'
Other boys present there soon joined them.

There was no reaction from Banshi. He stood resting his back to a tamarind tree, his vacant eyes hovering over the raging flames.

The night thickened and most of the people went back to their homes. Only a bunch of young men from the Mahanti -Lane sat around the fire, keeping vigil.

It was still dark when Dhruva reached the place where the bonfire was lit. The fire had died long since. Dhruva tried to remember how many potatoes he had flung into the fire last night. If fate favoured he might catch hold of one roasted brinjal or two if he kept groping a bit lard, he thought greedily. His mouth watered at the thought of eating soaked rice with the massed roasted potatoes and brinjals seasoned with crushed green chillies. A piece of onion to go along with that would double the taste. That was why he had come back to the place along with Dama and Gora before any one else had arrived.

The ash had heaped up to a hill. There must still be smouldering embers inside the ash. Dama got a piece of stick and began poking into the ash-heap. The stick touched some unusual object big and stiff. He poked more to see and suddenly jumped back screaming hard. It was a body ... a human body!! Someone has been burnt in the bonfire. His friends began screaming too and ran from the spot as fast as their feet took them off. The loud uproar invaded the sleeping houses and slowly people began to throng in. The village sarpanch arrived and with him came Rabi Malik, the village chowkidar. The police Inspector too arrived a little later. People of the neighbouring villages, gripped by curiosity joined the crowd. 'Who is that? Who has been burnt to death?' they kept asking one another.

'Look!' shouted Chandara, the son of Shyama the milkman. 'Here lies the Limping Banshi's lungi. But he is nowhere around.' The impact of the shocking discovery ran through the crowd like an electric wave. They looked for the Limping Banshi here, there and everywhere but did not find him. the police inspector concluded that it was Banshi's body charred beyond recognition. The body at last was identified. But why would the man, a cripple too, would enter the leaping flames?

'We had seen him last night. He stood leaning on the tamarind tree.' Dama and his friends Gora and Dhruv tried to be helpful. The elderly MadhuSantara confirmed it saying that he too had seen Banshi at the very spot while returning to his home.

'He was itching to die! Perhaps he had committed suicide by jumping into the fire.' The flock of young men of the Mahanti Lane scoffed. 'Good riddance!' another in the group muttered under his breath.

The strand of speculations stretched on and on, unstoppably. Imaginations ran wild portraying multiple scenes of Banshi falling into the fire. 'But what about his lungi that constantly slipped off his waist? Why is it lying here? What made Banshi strip himself naked before entering the fire?' Questions cluttered in the minds of the surprised onlookers.

'The man had not committed suicide. He was murdered!' declared the police inspector. ' Why would a man throw off his lungi before burning himself to death? Certainly not because he thought the lungi was more precious than his life!!'

The revelation came as a stunning blow to the speculating crowd.

'Exactly!! How come such an obvious fact had escaped us?' The whispering voices of the villagers went a pitch higher now. The line of discussions took a twist. Banshi the Lame now had settled stubborn in the thoughts of all the people, old and young. The picture that used to immediately flash before the eyes at the mention of 'Banshi the Lame' was one of a lanky and haggard man of ebony-black skin. More than half of his gaunt face was hidden in a shock of tousled beard. His head was capped by a tangled of mass wiry, windblown hair that was a disproportionate mix up of black and grey. The ribcage was distinctly outlined through the parchment like skin of his frail, bare chest.

He wore only a shabby lungi darned at several places loosely wound around the waist which slipped off time to time. He hitched it up and tightened the knot at the waist as many times as it slipped. It seemed as if he had no engagement other than gripping the lungi hard and knotting it a notch tighter.

There is an interesting but pathetic episode regarding how Banshi came to acquire the sobriquet of 'Banshi the Lame'. Grandmother used to narrate the incidents that led Banshi to live the life of a raddled beggar. Banshi was the only child of rich parents. His father was an affluent farmer owning large stretches of fecund farmland by the river side. The granaries were stuffed with sacks of paddy, and varieties of lentils. Besides the lands they owned six pairs of sturdy bullocks, about ten milch cows and other livestock including goats, sheep and hens. But fate had other plans for Banshi. There was an outbreak of cholera when Banshi was only four and both his parents succumbed to the deadly disease. The envious relatives and neighbours now had their coveted opportunity to grab the property that lawfully belonged to little Banshi. Bina Naik, vouching himself to be a distantly related uncle of Banshi offered to foster the orphaned Banshi and took the boy home. He got him admitted in the village primary school too. But after two years Banshi stopped attending school. He was instead sent to work in the crop-fields along with the other farmhands. He got into the company of the wicked cowherd boys and began stealing vegetables and fruits from the orchards and farmsteads of the villagers. Within a few years Banshi came to live with him, BinaNaik, by some fraudulent means got all Banshi's movable and immovable property legally transferred to his own possession reducing Banshi to a pauper in rags.

The accident occurred during the festival of Raja, while Banshi played the game of Kabadi. He had had a bad fall and injured one of his legs making him temporarily invalid. The leg healed slowly. But another disaster, much more severe than the first accident, struck the poor fellow before even his leg was completely healed. Banshi fell from a coconut tree while plucking coconuts and broke the other leg. There was a serious spinal injury too. No one in the village seriously cared to get him a timely medical attention. Nor did he have any money to pay for the treatment. He lay in his shack, writhing in pain till the wound became gangrenous. Finally he was taken to the hospital. But it was too late and the doctors advised am amputation. The portion under the knee of his right leg was amputated and Banshi was permanently crippled. People started calling him 'Banshi the Lame' and as days went by the sobriquet turned out to be his new identity.

Not all villagers despised Banshi. There were some who genuinely sympathized with him. Amongst the lot that wished well of him was Uttara, the daughter of SaniaPradhan. Banshi was a young man, and was handsome in an unpolished way. Uttara came to his hut when no one saw her. She brought him food and money without the knowledge of her parents. She tried to infuse confidence into him and persuaded him to come out of the state of morbid stagnancy, to do some physical exercise to bring life back to his stiff limbs. Uttara's encouraging words brought a faint glow to Banshi's bearded face. His tear-heavy eyes remained fixed for a while on her face and on the unflinching trust in her eyes and then roved over her body growing to the fullness of youth.

But the next moment his gaze travelled up to the vast bleak sky and then back to the road that went past his shack and lengthened out to some unknown destination. It was not easy to guess if Uttara could sense the tumult that surged within Banshi or could see the grave of unshed tears in his sunken eyes. She was always in a hurry to leave. She was afraid someone might discover her in Banshi's shack. She was afraid even to imagine the disaster that would follow the discovery. When Uttara left Banshi she also took back with her the tiny sparkles of hope that had lit had up Banshi's dark world for a brief moment. The fragile dream of his leg getting back to its normal condition was pulverised with the hard blow of reality. ' How long Uttara will come like this to my shack ? Will a day come when she will stop coming here?' the questions constantly nagged him. He was afraid to think about it. But one day his worst fears came true. Uttara got married and went away to live with her husband's family. Her absence made Banshi feel absolutely abandoned. He had to go without food most of the days. He became weak and frail. He went around begging and was often chased away mercilessly. People threw more contempt and pity than they offered food or any other form of help. And poor Banshi stomached it all. Day and night he prayed God to put an end to his cursed life. Storms and floods and even the super cyclone unleashed their fury on the village and claimed lives. But by some cruel joke of a hostile fate Banshi survived the disasters.

He was reduced to an object of ridicule, a clown. Children teased and tormented him with their nasty remarks just for the fun of it. Mothers made a bogey man of him to frighten their unruly kids. Banshi roamed about the village. During festivals he went from house to house begging for special dishes prepared for the occasion. Kids flung stones and the eyes of elders hurled abuses at him but he did not mind them. He just went limping about the village streets his hand gripping tightly the lungi that never seemed to stop slipping down his waist.

The police inspector continued his inquiry. He took people one by one and asked who had seen Banshi the lame for the last time or had spoken to him. It was Rahash, a young boy who finally offered the police the information. 'Around midnight Banshi had come to the spot where the bonfire was lit. Perhaps he wanted to grope in the fire and collect few roasted potatoes or brinjals from it. But the boys of Mahanty lane had sat around the fire, guarding. They were drinking alcohol. I heard them calling Banshi names. They opened his mouth forcibly and poured liquor down his throat. One of the boys pulled his lungi off and threw it to a distance. Not stopping at shouting obscenities at him the boys assaulted him physically. Banshi whined and wailed and begged them to let him go but they were under an alcoholic daze. In the end some boys lifted Banshi's naked body and flung him alive into the flames. Banshi yelled and howled at the top of his voice but the insane screaming of the boozed boys drowned his cries of agony. Rahash's parents pulled the boy away and quickly sneaked into an apparently lonely corner.

'What concrete evidence is there to affirm that the boys of our lane had burnt him to death?' BishiMahanty, a senior and respectable person of the Mohanty lane snapped. 'Could the words of this stupid boy be at all taken seriously?'

'Be ware! It will lead to serious consequences if anyone took the name of my son!' A woman pushed through the crowd to come out to the front. 'My son was amongst the others last night. But he was not the type to kill any one,' she declared.

'Times have changed. What is the harm in consuming a little spirit on festive occasions?' Some elderly people remarked defending the young men. 'They are young boys after all. Don't they have a right to revel on such occasions even in their own village?' The villagers turned to look accusingly at the parents of Rahash.

'Was that lame fellow one of your kinsperson? What business Rahash had to come forward and make a statement like that? A group of innocent young men would be arrested and put behind bars just because of a foolish statement made by a kid. Is it right?' Voices of dissension grew distinct and loud.

The Sarpanch pushed Rahash to one corner. 'Go and tell the Inspector that you have not seen or heard anything,' he hissed glaring at the boy.

'I haven't seen anything. I do not know anything. I just lied.' Keep rehearsing that and tell the police exactly that. Your family will be driven out of the village if you do not do as I ask,' the Sarpanch said menacingly.

'But they have thrown him into the fire. That is the truth. I have seen that in my own eyes' Rahash stammered, cringing in fear.

'You cannot see any truth any more once your eyes are pricked blind!' one of the stooges of the Sarpanch threatened. 'How would you like that?' Rahash looked at him fearfully. He too was there amongst the drunken lot, Rahash recognised. He too was involved in the crime. But Rahash had no alternative. He did as he was asked. The Sarpanch ,Rahash noticed, had succeeded in convincing the police Inspector through some crafty means.

But Rahash maintained a stubborn, unfazed silence when the inspector grilled him to extract information from him.

The police registered Banshi's death as an unnatural death, an accident. 'The victim had accidentally fallen into the fire and being physically disabled he was not able to save himself,' the report said. Before getting back to the police station the Inspector warned the Sarpanch to ban the festival of fire in future.

The villagers, one after other, left the place. The rowdies of the Mohanty lane, now relieved,   returned to their homes too.

Rahash stood alone, lost in the blinding darkness that obscured the path leading to his own insides. Something prodded him on and he ran after the police jeep that drove away leaving a cloud of dust behind.

What was Rahash exactly running after? Was it the police jeep, or the picture of Truth that was fading away fast from his sight?

●●

The Witch

I had never thought I would chance upon Shyam uncle in this place, and in this manner. As I stood across the counter of the medicine shop in the premises of the hospital to buy medicines and injections for my mother in law who had suffered a heart stroke and was admitted in that same hospital, a frail figure, who too stood at the counter, stretched out a gaunt hand that held a prescription, towards the chemist through the wicket of the counter. I would perhaps not have recognized him had he not startled me by calling me by my pet name.

'Minu!'

I turned to look at the man. His face looked vaguely familiar.

Who is this?

'Shyam uncle?'

What a transformation!! The Shyam uncle whom I remembered was a robust, fair complexioned, handsome man of more than six feet in height, who wore carefully trimmed moustaches. The man who called me Minu did not retain the slightest semblance of that aristocratic looks. His disheveled hair and unkempt beard had turned as white as snow and he was dressed in a shabby shirt and a pair of trousers that was not ironed. Could this be the same Shyam uncle who was so keen on maintaining his good looks and always wore perfectly pressed outfits that smacked off his aristocratic birth? What had brought in such a drastic change to his personality, and what about Nilima aunt, his wife? A number of questions tossed erratically about in my mind as I bent down to touch his feet.

'How are you, child? You have not changed a bit. Just grown up in height…'   My eyes moistened.

'Are you okay uncle? How is Nilima aunt?' I asked in return.

He suddenly looked devastated, as if a storm had blown past him. He stood still, and did not answer my questions. I too, did not want to press upon him. Perhaps he did not want to speak about Nilima aunt. He kept quiet, just the way he did on that evening before many years when the elderly members of the village convened a meeting to decide on the conduct of Nilima aunt. He spoke neither in favour of his elders nor of his wife.

'What are you doing here, child? Is someone sick…?' He asked without answering my questions.

'Yes, uncle. My mother in law is admitted here. She has had a heart surgery a few days back. She will be here for another week or so. She is in cabin number 122.'

'Cabin 122 ? Your aunt is in cabin 123.' Shyam uncle said.

I looked at him in surprise. Why is Nilima aunt in cabin no. 123? Why at all she is admitted in the hospital? 'Why is aunt admitted in the hospital? What happened?' I asked aloud.

'She is in coma. In fact she had suffered a massive paralytic stroke many years ago that had rendered her almost immobile. Now she has gone into a coma.'

'Nilima aunt had had a paralytic attack…! Since when?' I asked again.

'Her mind had stopped functioning normally since the day I brought her back here, after that meeting the elders of our village convened to denounce her conduct and virtually ostracized her. It had gravely affected her on psychological level. Later, she became a paraplegic, physically.'

I breathed out a deep sigh and walked up with him towards cabin number 123.

I could not believe my eyes. Nilima aunt lay tucked under a sheet. A number of tubes fitted to different parts of her body were connected to several electronic gadgets and monitoring screens. My mind refused to accept that this shriveled, pale figure under the sheet could be Nilima aunt, a woman who had a body that seemed hewn out of gold and a face that diffused a goddess-like radiance. Shyam uncle pulled a chair and asked me to sit down. He sat in another chair by the bed.

As I sat looking at the frail figure of the woman lying inert on the bed, who was once a stunning beauty, my thoughts travelled back years and years to the days of my childhood, when I lived with my parents and grandparents in our village.

The span of the four months that began with the day following the festival of Holi till the one that marked the end of the Raja, held a special significance for me. The school hours changed from daytime to morning which meant the sacrifice of the cozy, early morning sleep, a quick breakfast of soaked rice and mashed boiled-potatoes and rushing to the school. The long noontimes that followed the end of the school hours, however, were happy compensations that made the sacrifice worth it. Every day, I used to make different plans to spend the noontime in a satisfactory way, but there were a number of issues that happened to drastically impede the successful working out of my plans. Sometimes it was the restrictions imposed by my mother and my paternal aunt and sometimes the issues relating to my ailing grandfather's health. It was almost impossible to go out and play during the noon on the holidays and Sundays when father stayed at home. Despite all these hurdles, I managed to spend some of them in the way I wanted to.

During the noon hours, I and my two brothers Pintu and Chintu were made to sleep in the room at extreme end of the inner verandah. Mother warned us to go to sleep and went out to join the others who sat gossiping on the outer verandah. The cool breeze blowing from the south passed across the verandah and added to the charm of the experience of gossiping. The elderly Sashi aunt, Rama's mother, Sulei nani, and the comparatively younger Kuni bhauja were the ones that were regular participants in the meeting. Topping them all was Basanti aunt, famed as the village All India Radio, who used to preside over the meeting. My grandmother, after having her midday meal would be reclining on a flax-mat on the outer verandah. The women, one after another would make their way there. My mother would clean the kitchen, wash the used utensils and then go out to join them. I would be waiting straining my ears to pick up the clanging of the utensils as mother after cleaning them kept them in an upended position. I knew that after keeping back the washed utensils mother would come to the outer verandah carrying the betel-basket. And then the lid of the mysterious casket of gossip would open and curious and strange and palatable information would hop out of it. The temptation to eavesdrop and share mysterious talks the women exchanged was almost irresistible. Summer was the season of the ripening of the mangoes. I could have, as an alternative to this secret adventure, gone to the mango grove and collected the ripe and half-ripe mangoes that had dropped from the trees. But that was the choice I could have opted for only when the subject of the talk amongst the women was not palatable and spicy to hold me in a spell. There happened once a very unpleasant incident. As I stood listening to the women talking, hiding from their eyes, my elder paternal aunt caught sight of me. She came up to me, landed a couple of heavy blows on my back and pulling me by my arm, brought to this room at the extreme end of the verandah, pushed me in and closed the door from outside. 'Call me through the window if you need to take a pee' she said and went away. My mother too admonished me for not taking a nap during the noon. She said that to sleep for a while during noontime would help me since I had to get up early in the morning to attend the morning school. But my aunt was in the habit of drawing her own conclusions. 'The character of someone could be judged from one's childhood manners. This habit of secretly listening to the talks of the adults is not a sign of a good character.' My mother listened to the allegations without saying anything. There was a look in her eyes that could mean anything from an apprehension that I was developing bad habits, to an accusation that it was for me that she had to bear such humiliation. Perhaps there was a feeble protest, like 'She was just a child. She had no intention to eavesdrop. She came to stand there just because she was not feeling sleepy.' But it held a strange pathos which compelled me to confine myself to the bed most of the days.

But it was too trying to hold back the overpowering interest to hear about the gossips involving Para, the wife of a farmer, and Nilima aunt. Between the two the later was more tempting, because I had a special attachment for Nilima aunt. She was Shyam uncle's wife. Shyam uncle, a tall, handsome young man with a princely look, hailed from the extraordinarily rich Chhotray family, a family that had an aristocratic ancestry. He was the only son of his parents. His wife, Nilima aunt, a stunningly beautiful woman, had a complexion like burnished gold. She had large expressive eyes and her face always wore a radiant smile. A large vermilion spot on her forehead dazzled like a rising sun. She was not only an educated woman but a very affectionate person too. She always fed us with different sorts of delicacies whenever we went to her house. On festive occasions like Raja and Kumar Purnima, she combed our hair, made braids and tied them with colourful ribbons. She made designs with sandalwood paste on our forehead and painted our feet with alta. Besides these, Nilima aunt also helped me in solving the difficult problems of arithmetic. There was something else that drew me to Nilima aunt's house time and again. Nilima aunt was an avid reader of books and neatly stacked on the shelves in her bedroom were novels, short story collections and many other interesting books. I used to borrow books from her and return them to her after reading.

I could not accept easily what Basanti Aunt said about her.

'Shame on her!' Basanti aunt was saying. 'And to hell with her educational qualification!! What is the meaning of all that education if she conducted herself in this deplorable manner?'

The secret of the farmer-wife Para which Basanti aunt disclosed had surprised the women. But what Basanti aunt said relating to Nilima aunt's nature and conduct seemed to have dropped a bombshell. And no one had the opportunity to verify the truth.

'Are you sure Nani? Have you seen it for yourself?'
I could hear my mother asking innocently,
'It is the only topic that is discussed everywhere in the village', Basanti aunt said, her voice convincingly assertive.
Shyam uncle and Nilima aunt did not live in the village. They used to pay short visits to the ancestral house during festival times or some such occasions. Shyam uncle left Nilima aunt in village for a few days' stay and then took her back to the town. I and my friends loved to spend time with her during those days.

'You should not let your daughter to go to Nilima's house,' Basanti aunt used to warn my mother. 'A glance from her evil eye would suck the sap out of the child!'

My mother said nothing in reply, nor did she forbid me from visiting Nilima aunt. Nilima aunt was a decent woman. She never came to the outer verandah nor had anybody ever seen her without a veil draped over her head. The reason why Basanti aunt disliked her was that she had not had any issue. People in the village had formed diverse opinions relating to the fact. Some called Shyam uncle impotent. That was the reason why he could not beget aunt a child. And the depression resulting out of the realization had led his mother to a premature death. But most people blamed Nilima aunt for the deficiency. In a male dominated society like ours, it is the woman who has to bear the brunt of baseless accusations in such matters. It could not be that something of such discussions hadn't have reached Nilima aunt's ears, but she maintained a placid silence.

And then, something happened that gave me the real shakes!

On that particular noon, as I stepped out of the gate of Nilima aunt's house, Basanti aunt, God knows from where, appeared suddenly and before I could say anything in defense, catching my right arm in a vice grip, dragged me towards our house. Standing in front of our house she yelled at my grandma and my mother.

'It seems you people will learn only when the child dies!' She said loudly. 'Why do you allow her to go to that witch? Yes, she *is* a witch. She has a big black mole on her tongue. In the darkness of the nights she escapes to the cremation ground, fully naked and moves about, walking on her palms, head down and legs up, eating human defecations. The daughter-in law of the Patra family had gone to visit that witch taking her one year old son with her, the other day. The witch took the baby in her arms, and kissed it. The baby suffered from high fever and died by midnight. They buried the baby in the cremation ground. Towards the last part of night, some people saw this witch sitting by a fire by the baby's grave, her legs stretched forward and was warming the dead baby with the heat of the flame. They began running for their lives. The news spread around the village faster than a wildfire. How long the truth can be kept concealed? Now it had come out to the open as was obvious.' I stood there, gaping at Basanti aunt, badly caught in between belief and disbelief.

'She is coming frequently to the village leaving her husband alone in their house in the town to make her sinister nocturnal visits to the crematory grounds since she is not finding ample opportunity there to do so', Basanti aunt went on unstoppably. Mother signaled me to go inside and I, despite my overwhelming curiosity to listen what she would say next, had to leave the place. But the shocking revelation stole sleep away from my nights. I lay awake in the bed, till late into the night, turning the subject over and over in my mind. 'Is there any truth in what Basanti aunt had said? Is it true that Nilima aunt is a witch? That she has a large black mark on her tongue that is the sign of a witch? That she moves in the crematory ground at night and eats human defecation? That she sucks the life-blood out from little children with her evil glance?' My thoughts were in a turmoil, and I was sure I could not rest till I checked the truth of all these.

But how?

I could not ask Nilima aunt directly. It was unthinkable to hide myself somewhere in the thickets near the crematory ground in the night and keep a watch over her movements.

After Basanti aunt's warnings, my grandmother began keeping a strict guard over me. My mother was not that rigid but she did not encourage me. The restriction imposed on me had deprived me of the pleasure which the novel and story books from her shelves used to bring to me. I was, however, all the time in the lookout for an opportunity to slip out to Nilima aunt's house and check out the truth of what Basanti aunt said about Nilima aunt having a large black mole on her tongue.

And, at last, it came in my way. I managed to escape the vigilant eyes of my grandmother and stole out of the house. Nilima aunt was resting. She got off the bed and came out to greet me smiling her bright, happy smile. 'I was missing you a lot! To see you daily has become a routine thing for me, ' she said, embracing me. I kept gaping at her face smiling stupidly, almost willing her to open her mouth a little wider so that I could have a good look at her tongue. I walked up to the bookshelf, pretending to search books of my choice. 'Aunt,' I said moving towards the kitchen, 'Didn't have you any sweets for me today?' Immediately she lifted the lid of a jar and taking out a coconut ladoo from it, put it in my mouth.

'Take the whole jar of the ladoos while going back,' Nilima aunt said affectionately. 'I have made them for you only.' I saw my chance. 'Of course, I will take the ladoos, but you will have to eat one from my hand,' I said holding up a ladoo to her open mouth. I took a look at her tongue and my eyes caught sight of a big black patch on her tongue. My hand remained suspended in midair, and I felt a cold shiver creeping through me. I shoved the ladoo into her mouth. 'I had left my notebooks open on the table by the window,' I said anxiously.' I don't know if anyone would have put them back in the shelf. I must rush back to see,' I said and without waiting for Nilima aunt's reply hurried out of her house. I ran as fast as my legs could carry me and on reaching home went straight to the last room on the end of the verandah and flopped on the bed. My mind was a battle field of warring thoughts. Did the black mole on Nilima aunt's tongue testify to the fact that she was a witch, as Basanti aunt had told? Did she suck the blood out of infants? Did she, stripping herself bare, walk with her hands in the cremation ground and lick at the human excretions? I felt my mind was split into two, one part wanting to believe Basanti aunt and the other vehemently denying it. The captivating, charming personality of Nilima aunt did not match even distantly, with the gruesome and grotesque image of the witch who conducted herself, according to Basanti aunt, in such a horrid manner!!

'She is such a evil woman!' Basanti aunt used to add to her observations on Nilima aunt, 'She comes to the village again and again leaving her husband, who is a gem of a man, just because she has to have her freedom to carry on with her loathsome habit! She must not be allowed to continue this gruesome practice. It has to be brought to the notice of the seniors of the village and the matter be placed before the Village *Panchayat* (the five member committee that adjudicates the issues of the people of the village).'

It was only old Udiya grandpa, the most respected character of the village, who could bring the matter to the *Pachayat*. He had to be alerted first!

As the days moved past the tales of Nilima aunt being a witch spread out to almost every house in the village. The air was thick with suspicion and anger. If Nilima aunt had any inkling of the rumor that was spreading fast around the village, it did not show in her behaviour.

Ultimately, as it was expected, the inevitable happened. The tale found its way to old Udiya grandpa's ears. The witch-episode was bound to take an ugly twist and reach its disastrous climax. Udiya grandpa brought the matter to the notice of the *Panchayat*. Shyam uncle was called back from the town. The members of the committee discussed the issue in his presence but Shyam uncle did not say anything either in favour of or against his wife, he just sat there silently while people slashed at the imagined-evil in his own wife. His unusual silence complicated the matter and made it difficult for the members to arrive at any decision relating to the subject.

'Shame upon him,' remarked a few after the meeting was over. 'He is such a uxorious husband! Not uttered even a word during the meeting!'

The next day, Shyam uncle left for the town taking Nilima aunt with him. They never returned. The front doors of his large house never opened again. Natia Teli, who was entrusted with the charge of keeping the house, had a heyday. He along with others caught the fish in their pond, took away all the coconuts and areca nuts from the orchards, and literally plundered the property. The house, wearing an abandoned, rundown look, stood silently like a pathetic apparition of an aristocracy that had given Shyam uncle and his family their distinguished status.

'Your aunt was not a witch! It was I who had imaged her as one before the people of the village!'

Shyam uncle said, and I was jolted back to the present time.

I stared him blankly, not being able to make anything out of what he said.

'Meaning?'

'Your Nilima aunt was fond of kids. But she could not conceive a baby. It was not her fault though. The defect was in me. But the man in me and his ego held me back from admitting it. Instead, I kept blaming her, making her feel responsible for everything. I drowned myself in alcohol to come out of the frustration and my sense of guilt. Nilima, too, passed through a terrible ordeal. She blamed herself for our childlessness. Her sense of loss combined with my drinking habit developed an irritability in her. She wanted to live in the village. When it became unbearable for her to put up with my accusing temperament and my alcoholic spree, she decided to go back to the village for good.

But I did not want her leave here, and thought of a plan to create a situation that would compel her to leave the village. I went to an astrologer whom I knew and sought his advice. I could, with his help, convince Nilima that there was a way which could beget her a child. She had to collect some earth from the place in the crematory ground where an infant was buried, keep it an amulet and wear it. I knew that it was all rubbish. But it would serve a two-fold purpose. First, Nilima would realize that I was as eager to have a baby as she was, and second, her abnormal conduct would certainly come to the notice of someone in the village. She would be thought of an witch and would be permanently banished from there. I had no patience with the people in the village who exasperated me with constant queries regarding our childlessness.

But Nilima had great faith in astrology, and she never doubted my words. She readily agreed to act as advised by the astrologer. My evil scheme worked out successfully and, as I had wanted, our visits to the village were permanently stopped. But I had not had the slightest inkling that the consequences would be so disastrous.

Nilima had changed drastically. She did not speak a word, nor did she react to anything. She even could not cook food properly. Sometimes she put sugar in the curry in place of salt and tea dust in the rice pot. I took her to a psychiatrist. 'She is under the impact of some terrible mental shock,' the doctor diagnosed. She was placed under treatment but nothing helped to restore her mental balance. Things got worse and after sometime her brain got partially paralyzed.'

Uncle paused briefly. I did not say anything. The unexpectedness of the revelation had made me speechless.

'I have been passing through sheer hell. It is much more than what she had suffered. Perhaps this the punishment for the sin I had committed, and I had got it in *this* life!' Shyam uncle said in a small voice, as if he was speaking to himself.

I looked at him. There were no tears in his eyes. Perhaps, he too, like Nilima aunt, had forgotten to shed them. There was a pale glitter in place of it.

Was it remorse?

Was it penitence? Penance?

I was not sure!!

●●

Claw

Shibu cried even more, his sobs lingering to a wavy trail of whimpers.

'Shut up you fool!' Aju warned. 'Be quiet or Rakaa dada will storm in and thrash you. He might even hack a leg or a hand off like he had done to Ranjan and Pintu. He is a monster without a grain of pity in him. The only thing he cares about is money, and only money.'

Aju tried to comfort the little boy who had arrived in the den just last night. But Shibu kept on with his whining, panting under the impact of the choking sobs.

With this new arrival the number of the boys in Rakaa dada's gang had gone up to fourteen. Aju is the leader of this gang, not because he was older in age than the others but because he was the oldest member and the most trusted of Rakaa dada. He had that quality to convince the other kids and win over them.

But Shibu was implacable. 'I want to go to my mother,' he went on and on amidst the sobs that wracked his small form. Aju had been trying all possible methods within his reach to stop him from crying but had not succeeded. 'I want to go to my mother,' the boy kept on like he was singing a litany.

'Can anyone find a way back to one's mother once

he reaches here?' Aju thought despairingly. He himself had come to this place in a truck. Could he find a way out to make a return? He was eight when he came here. He was seventeen now. He had spent nine long years here, working for Rakaa dada.

He had seen eight kids dying. Every time one of them had died he had gone through the tearing agony of losing someone of his own. John and Vinaya had come with him. Both of them died within a year. John succumbed to fever. Vinaya was beaten to death. He refused to obey Rakaa dada and demanded to be sent back to his home. Malini didi and Rakaa dada both tried hard to bring him to line, but Vinaya was obstinate and bold. Rakaa dada had broken one of his legs. But neither Rakaa's demonic looks nor his beatings could intimidate Vinaya enough to lie low. Furious at this blatant obstinacy, Rakaa beat the boy to death.

Aju knew that Malini didi was no kin of Rakaa dada. She was not even distantly related to him. She gave him massages and slept with him. Every morning she made the kids stand in a file, counted their number to ascertain that no one had run away. She warned them never to try to make an escape. She suggested the menu to Kanta Amma, the cook-cum-domestic help and at times supervised the cooking. She threatened the kids trying to bring an angry glare to her eyes, but she did not have that diabolic ferocity in her eyes.

Truth to be told, Malini didi too never had any genuine love for Raka Dada. She too, like the fourteen boys and girls, was a captive in Raka Dada's jail. But she had nowhere to go. The lecherous boys hanging around the traffic signal had their dirty eyes on her. But none of them dared to say anything to Malini didi because she was in Rakaa dada's protection.

Raka dada looked horrible, Aju thought disdainfully. One of his eyes was perhaps plucked out in some brawl with somebody. His ugly face was covered with a number of large and deep cut marks. There was no index finger in his right hand. Must be the consequences of some other fight. All these put together gave him a look of a real devil!

Aju had often noticed Malini didi shedding tears when she was alone. Why did she weep? Aju wondered. Did she weep because she missed her home, her family? And where were her parents? Her home?

These days Malini didi blushed when she saw Aju looking at her.

'You have become a big boy!' She remarked, looking closely at him. Aju shrank within in embarrassment. A shiver ran through him when Malini didi touched him.

Pinki, Sneha and Kunti had now fallen preys to Raka dada's devouring lust. Raka dada entered his bedroom every night with one of the girls. Malini didi cursed him, every time he did that.

'This blood hound will not spare any one,' she grumbled. 'He would lick away everything with his dirty tongue.' Malni didi could not bear the thought of the lives of those innocent girls getting ruined.

That is how Bithi had died.

She was only twelve. She was beautiful and Rakaa's favourite. He called her Gori (fair complexioned) and did not let her go begging like other kids in the group. After sending all the others out Rakaa spent hours and hours alone with Bithi in the shack. There was not a single night he had let her alone. He kept on clawing her even when she got pregnant with his baby. He had planned to put the baby in the racket. He knew that an infant cradled in the arm of a poor woman would be a better source of profit in his business. The pains came eventually and Rakaa called a midwife. But Bithi succumbed to the pain. The baby too died in her womb. Rakaa threw Bithi's dead body into the river in the darkness of the night. No one had the slightest inkling where Bithi suddenly disappeared. But Malini didi knew and she had told Aju.

Malini didi shared many such secrets with Aju. Aju wondered why she trusted him.

Shibu started whimpering once again. Malini didi ran in. 'Hey! Stop it!' She held Shibu tightly in her arms and warned. 'The villain has come back. The rogue does not have even a little mercy in his heart. God knows what he will do to you if he got angry.' She put a piece of bread into Shibu's mouth, but Shibu had no interest in food. Nor did he feel hungry. The only thing he wanted was to go back to his mother.

The three boys, Shibu, Rajiv and Aakash had arrived there last night. Shibu was the youngest, five or six perhaps. He looked cuddly and cute. Rakaa dada had asked to keep him without food for a few days. Starving would reduce him to bones and he would draw more sympathy from the people. More sympathy meant more earning. Rakaa had not made his decisions about Akash and Rajiv. God only knew what fate had stored for those two! Malini's heart went out to the poor kids.

Akash, the son of a homeopathic doctor, was studying in class four in an English medium school. He bought an ice cream on the way while returning from the school. He sucked at the ice cream and everything went blank. When he came back to his senses he discovered him here, in Rakaa dada's den.

Rajib, ate candy floss from the old vendor while returning from the playground and had passed out. He had no money but the old man volunteered to give him the candy floss for free. He was brought here unconscious, along with Shibu and Akash. He could neither remember nor understand how he came here.

But Aju understood. He knew how Rakaa's human trafficking racket functioned.

All criminals like Rakaa had identified the traffic post where they let their respective gangs operate. No one trespassed into the other's area. Rakaa commanded ownership over five such traffic signals. Aju knew that the more the number of kids, the more will be the turnover. But the number was not the only factor that guaranteed more earning. The kids had to be disabled, maimed, and disfigured to draw attention and sympathy from the people.

Aju also knew those who worked for Rakaa. There was Ramjaan chacha, the ice cream vendor. He sold drugged ice creams to the children. There were Rustam uncle, Dhiraj bhai, Abanti Bai and old man Kashi. All of them lived in different towns and remained in the lookout for opportunity for snatching little children. Abanti bai sold utensils of steel in exchange of old clothes. She had access to most of the houses and got close to the family members. All the time she kept an alert eye on the houses and the family living therein. She tried to find out how many children lived in each house and collect other useful information. Old man Kashi sold candy floss and lozenges near a school. He too kept his sharp gaze fixed on easy preys. Rustam uncle hawked stationary items. He carried his merchandise on his bicycle and moved in the alleys and lanes, got friendly with the people of all ages and used them as his source of information.

Dheeraja bhai, the auto-rickshaw driver was in the charge of transportation of the kids. He put the unconscious children in his rickshaw and later sent them either in a pickup van or a truck to be delivered at Rakaa's shack. Rakaa decided the price after appraising the catches. But, however promising the victim might seem the rate never exceeded five thousand.

It was not only Rakaa dada who ran such a racket. All the kids who begged at different traffic signals, were kidnapped from different places. A uniform pattern was followed by the racketeers to train them. They were not sent to work immediately. In the first few days of their arrival they were kept confined in the den. Then they were tortured and threatened. In the end they were given drugs. That was the one thing that worked wonders. Once the kids got addicted to drugs, they would never want to escape. That was when they were sent out to work.

Last year Rakaa dada had hacked off Rajan's leg, just below the knee. Aju could never dismiss the horrific memory from his system. 'A boy without a leg inspires more pity,' Rakaa dada would explain. 'It is an unfailing marketing strategy in the begging-world.'

So, Rakaa had slashed Pintu's arm off and burnt the tongue of Mahesh by shoving smouldering charcoal into the boy's mouth. The dumb, deformed and the maimed ones had always been the guarantee for better dividends.

Compounder Aftab, a close associate of Rakaa treated the wounds. He had his commission fixed.

'Doctor, my foot!!' Malini didi said, her voice thick with loathing. 'Bloody quack!!'

Now and then a flame of blind rage sparked off in Aju's heart. He even contemplated murdering the villain Rakaa and putting an end to his devilish act, once and for all. Now and then the police too came to the shack acting upon some informer's report. Malini didi hid the children on those occasions and played 'the innocent wife' of Rakaa before the police. Aju could not help but admire Malini didi's performance before the police.

There were times when Aju thought he would go to the police and tell them the truth. That was perhaps the only way to escape this hell, he thought. But he could not bring his plan to action. There was that thing which held him back. The white powder! The white powder had cast such a spell over the children that they had forgotten everything about their past. They had forgotten even who they really were. The white powder was what Malini didi called 'drugs' and what was Rakaa's invincible weapon to keep the kids under absolute control.

There were days when Aju remembered his own family, his home. But, try as he might , he could not remember the name of the town or village his home was. He remembered his parents and Rinki, his younger sister, but the faces appeared so blurred that it was difficult to identify them. Sometimes a hazy picture of the backyard of his home or the well his mother drew water from in pitchers came to his mind. He could vaguly recollect a cement platform there on which his father sat puffing at his bidi after he had fed the cows in the cowshed. There were a few hens too. His mother kept the eggs for Aju. 'My son would go stronger eating them', she used to say.

Malini didi said that his real name was Rajesh. Aju did not bother to know if it was true. Surprisingly enough, he still remembered the name of his sister, Rinki, though he had forgotten her face.

There was a dance stage in his village, Aju remembered faintly. Every summer, during the festival of *Raja*, *pala* singers used to perform there. During the *Dola* festival, plays were enacted there and operas on the occasion of

Sitalsasthi. He also remembered playing the character of Sudama in the opera *KamsaBadha* .

There was a huge pond at the end of the village where lilies bloomed in profusion. Aju's mother warned him repeatedly not to enter the pond. There were snakes in the pond, she said. But Aju ignored and went into the water to pluck the lilies for the worshipping of the goddess *Mangala* in the happy autumns. To dive into the pond with other boys, swimming far to collect the lilies had turned into an obsession those days.

Aju wondered how could he, in this brief span of eight years, forget almost everything about himself!!

This white powder had ruined his life, his happiness, even his memory, Aju admitted gloomily to himself. He got crazy to have a little of that powder, his ticket to the land of luxurious forgetfulness. All the children craved for that delicious poison the way he did. It was only when Rakaa dada returned and gave them each a pinch of that powder that their desperateness was put to rest.

'That powder is Rakaa's magic wand. How could he otherwise have managed to keep you all tethered to one single post, in one fold?'

Aju kept planning different ways to get free from Rakaa's clutch but could never put his plans to action. He used to forget the next moment what had he planned. He knew that it was the impact of the drugs. His addiction had crippled him, drained out all his energy. A strange sluggishness seeped into him which slowed down the workings of his mind too. But he did not have the will power to fight this indomitable urge.

There were a few occasions when he had become physical with Malini didi. She shifted closer and closer to him and let her sari fall off her breasts, trying to arouse him. Aju could not resist her. He noticed a glow of some mysterious happiness on Malini did's face the next morning. But Aju could not recollect clearly what had happened last night. He was yet to come out of the hangover.

Rakaa dada never objected to it. He knew he would need Malini and Aju both if he had to keep his business running. He did not want to hurt either of them. He was rather having a good time with the three girls, Pinki, Kunti and Sneha. He never let them alone despite Malini didi's objections.

But Malini didi could not tolerate when Rakaa entered his room taking eight year old Chinu with him. She stopped him, reacting vehemently.

'The poor baby will die. Leave her alone,' she warned. After a long debate with Malini, finally Raka agreed to let Chinu go. But Aju knew that Raka still had his eyes on Chinu. He could do anything to her if he found her alone, without Malini didi to protect her. 'What a monster!' Aju was filled with revulsion.

Malini didi sat holding Shibu on her lap, mopping his face with her sari. Her bosom was bared of cover. Aju's gaze kept on travelling back and forth to her breasts. Malini didi was older than him by a few years and Aju knew that eyeing her youth in this way was improper. He tried to avert his gaze but the effort proved too much.

'What is there in the age?' Malini didi used to argue. 'The one thing that counts is the heart ... if your heart admits and your soul permits age could never be an impending factor.' She adds.

'May be she is right!' Aju thought doubtfully. But he too was often driven by a desire to lose himself in her! He could not stop himself from getting close to Malini didi. He loved the experience, though he was prompted more by the influence of the drug than his conscious will. Malini didi would press Aju's cheeks fondly before she wrapped her sari around her bare body. Aju kept eyeing her nudeness hungrily, wondering how could a woman's body be so intoxicating, so fragrant and so hot!!

Malini didi smiled at him knowingly. Aju waited for the 'next time' and another 'next time' thereafter... and slowly it fell into a habit.

Things have a way of falling into a habit. Just like to act like a beast had become a habit with Rakaa dada. Just like he had fallen into the habit of growing increasingly brutal! And, just like he had fallen into the habit of mauling the tender girls and disfiguring and disabling the kids by hacking off their limbs, or plucking out their eyes!!

Every day, every hour these heinous crimes occurred in this city. The number of crippled children kept growing at the traffic signals. People turned a blind eye to them. Some of them, moved by sympathy, threw a coin into their desperate hands and went about in their business. Life raced on an ever lengthening road, indifferent to the pains of these suffering souls for whom time had stood still at one single point.

One day Shibu ran away. Nobody knew where to.

In a frenzy of frustration Rakaa dada plucked one of Rajiv's eyes and hacked Akash's palm off.

Where did the little Shibu go? Aju wondered. 'He might have fallen a prey to another Rakaa dada, or have got caught in the fatal snare of the criminals who ran the human kidney-trafficking racket.'

'Some apparently kindhearted fellow would have taken him to his house and making him work as a domestic help.' There was even another worst possibility which Aju wanted to banish from his thoughts, but which kept creeping in. 'Shibu might have come under some automobile and...!!'

Would he be living a life that was worth living even after escaping this hell? Aju thought dubiously. A few drops of tears trickled down his eyes.

At long last he made a decision. He would himself look for Shibu. He would go to every possible place where Shibu had a chance to escape to. He would put all his effort in finding out the boy. And once he did find him, Aju decided, he would leave him at the police station. It was thereafter the responsibility of the police to send Shibu back to his home. Aju would not show himself to the police but would tell the truth if at all the police caught him.

Aju was in two minds whether or not he should speak to Malini didi about it.

Malini didi was sitting on the verandah. She looked dull and pale.

Aju walked to her and sat down, close to her.

'Where did Shibu go?' he asked.

'Who knows?' Malini replied absently.

'He might not have gone far,' Aju said. 'He must be very much here , in this city. Should we try to find him and then take him to the police station? He was so small. Let at least one of us be saved from the claws of crime. Let him go back to his parents!'

Malini turned to look straight at Aju. There was a strange glint in her eyes.

'Are you serious? Will you really leave him with the police if you find him? Are you telling the truth?'

Malini didi's anxious voice was a blend of fear and astonishment.

'Absolutely! Trust me!'

'Come with me,' Malini stood up and held Aju's

hand. After walking a mile or so they reached at the shack of the domestic help-cum-cook, Kantha Amma. Shibu was playing marbles with Kantha Amma's grandson. The old woman was startled to find Aju there.

'Don't fear. He is not in Rakaa dada's camp. He is with us.' Malini assured Kantha Amma.

Aju took Shibu's tiny hand in his own and headed towards the police station.

●●

The Victory Beat

The sound drew closer and closer.

The rhythmic beats of the drum got more and more distinct and clear.

It filled Sadananda with a strange disquiet. He sat on the outer veranda leaning against the wall. But as the sound moved closer he sprang up to his feet and paced up and down the veranda. An intense overpowering mood compelled him to give in to an indefinable restlessness.

Sadananda was close on eighty. His eyesight was failing fast. Still, sparkling waves of triumph and a hitherto unfelt sense of the joy of achieving something unachievable rose and broke along his old sunken eyes.

His skin had turned brittle like parchment. Ailments that accompany old age had given him a pale and sickly look. But he had neither let his hope waver nor the dream that haunted his sleep regularly for the long, unending years, fade.

He was as if waiting, his ears pricking, to hear this sound for years on end! For more than half a century!

The drums were beating, nonstop. The sound was approaching fast. People of all ages have come outdoors from the neighbouring houses to watch the procession. Finally, Sadananda thought with satisfaction, the court had given a decree in his favour. He had put all his resources, his effort, his time into this civil suit, and had won the case. He had got back the ownership of his four acres of ancestral land unlawfully denied to him by his cousins. He had recovered his right to his property and his self-esteem. It was not a legal suit for him, Sadananda reflected proudly. It was an obsession. It was a lone battle he fought with eleven families. It was not a small achievement to fight such an uneven battle for more than fifty years and emerge victorious!! Tears of joy rolled down his eyes that sparkled under the spectacles.

He turned to look about. His own family had gathered on the veranda waiting for the victory procession. Everyone was there, his son, his daughter-in-law, his grandchildren and even the houseboys and maids and the farmhands. The only one missing was Sumitra, his wife. She should have been the first one to come out to watch. She should have stood by his side in the battle ground where he fought for his right. Her absence did not surprise Sadananda, though, it was, on the other hand, his son who extended his unflinching support to him in his war against injustice.

Sadananda took a deep breath. He did not blame Sumitra. How could she feel the humiliation of being deprived of one's own rightful possessions? How could she experience the agony of being rendered homeless? May be it was not proper on his part to expect absolute empathy from her, he reasoned. Sadananda was not listening to the beats of the victory-drum now. Another sound, from the distant but living past, the sound of the pitiful whining of two kids had drowned it. He could distinctly hear both he and his five year old younger brother crying loudly. There was another woebegone voice that merged in to it, that of his own elder sister , a child widow of eleven. Even after all these years he could see everything clearly, with every minute detail, as if the scene was being replayed before his eyes. The scene of a girl of eleven and her two brothers, one of nine and the other five, being mercilessly thrown out to the road flashed before his eyes with a rare vividness.

His mother had succumbed to cholera. Father followed her soon. Everything was so sudden and so simple, like the bubble burst. There were times when Sadananda doubted if at all it was actually cholera his mother had died of. His elder sister, given away in marriage when she was just seven had been widowed at ten and came back to live with her parents. It was a terrible shock. Perhaps, Sadananda reflected ruefully, it was too much an effort for his poor mother to survive the trauma. Sadananda's grandfather, the eldest of the three brothers, had only one son. This only son was the father of Sadananda. The two younger grandfathers had total eleven sons and seven daughters. After the death of Sadananda's parents the eleven sons had ganged up to usurp all the properties of Sadananda's father and his home too.

The three kids, orphaned, bereft of a shelter, were now on the streets, starving and struggling to survive. Sadananda was scared to recollect the pain and sufferings and the struggles they had to put up with during those days of abject distress. They slept on the verandas of different neighbours on different nights and slaked their hunger with the fruits growing in the unfrequented wilderness. His sister had to work as a housemaid in people's houses. She pounded paddy at the husking pedal and sometimes babysat too. All that exhausting manual labour began to take toll on her health. She grew frailer by the day. The social stigma attached to the image of a widow and the strict regulations imposed on a widow's conduct and living pattern too played no less important a role in deteriorating her both mentally and physically.

Even at that tender age of nine Sadananda could understand life with all its complexities. It is rightly believed that circumstances could teach a person many important lessons. Circumstances make one matured before time while another enjoys the luxury of living an easy and carefree life all through. Circumstances compelled Sadananda to seek a living at distant Calcutta leaving his village. His sister, however, was not sold on the idea. But there was no other alternative available.

The hostile indifference of the villagers, the jibes of friends and relatives challenged all limits of his forbearance. Many from the village, at that time, were working at Calcutta earning a good living. Sadananda decided to try his luck there. So he came to Calcutta with some other people of his village. An elderly person of the village helped Sadananda to get a job of a houseboy in a Bengali family. His employer was a good fellow. In a few months Sadananda worked as a cook there, with an increased salary. He found time to continue his studies too. Later, he brought his younger brother to Calcutta and got him the job of a houseboy in another family. His sister lived alone in the village in a two-room clay-walled house. Every month Sadananda sent money to her sister, who lived alone in the village, by money order. The money, however, did not always reach his sister. Sometimes the sly post peon gypped it and took his sister's fingerprint on the receipt without making any payment to her. Sadananda did not have a means to verify if at all his sister was receiving the money he sent. He came home only once in a year.

At early morning one day a man from the village

came to his employer's house to give him the news of his sister's death. His sister had strangled herself to death a month back, the man told boy Sadananda who felt like the sky crashing down on him. Her body was not cremated but the villagers had thrown it on the cremation ground for the scavengers to feast on. And such a heinous crime was committed in the presence of the village watchman who stood as a mute witness.

The shock had turned Sadananda to stone.

How could God be so cruel to sanction so much sorrow, so much pain to his lot?

But he tried to exercise control over his sinking heart. He gathered carefully the scatters of his life falling in an ugly clamour.

He continued to work as a cook in families, carried on with his studies and went from house to house selling books to earn some extra money. He hawked newspapers in the early morning hours. He got through the school finals successfully.

It was as if at last God cast a merciful glance in his direction. He got an appointment in the Railway department. His younger brother had gone back to village after their sister's death. He lived in the village doing all and sundry jobs. Sadananda sent money to his brother regularly. Life was finally turning corner.

The embers of anger caused by the hurt and the humiliations, the terrible pangs of suffering that had remained buried under an ash-heap for years sparked off to a blazing flame. Sadananda filed a lawsuit in the court to get back his right over the property which was wrested out from him by his paternal uncles.

Once started, the process went on endlessly, year after year. Sadananda had married in the meantime and now his son had become an adult of forty five years. His daughters too had been given away in marriage long years back. Sadananda had now college-going grandchildren. But the court case continued.

Sadananda's son was an enterprising boy. He was appointed in a government office that paid well. It was his son who always stood by him. He had given him unquestioning moral and financial support in Sadananda's battle against injustice. He had been Sadananda's strength, the leverage that always lifted his tilting spirit. As if he had taken a pledge to fulfil his father's wish for victory, to see the battle through till its end.

The one thing that pricked at Sadananda's heart now and then, was the lack of cooperation from his wife Sumitra. Sumitra was an ideal life partner. She had sacrificed all her comfort and happiness to run the household unhindered. In the hours of financial crisis she had unflinchingly let him pawn and sell her scanty jewellery to meet the domestic expenses. But, Sadananda failed to understand why she did not stand by him in the most important and meaningful battle of his life. He failed to understand why she did not respect his decision to fight for his legitimate claim!!

He turned to look at the inner courtyard. Sumitra was sitting by the cutting-board. There was a vague look in her eyes. She sat there mindlessly cutting the vegetables. Sadananda wondered if at all the sound of the drumbeats reached her ears. He wanted to call her loudly, but stopped himself. He knew that Sumitra would reiterate her old arguments. She would say that it was not right to deprive someone of a property which had remained under his possession for nearly sixty to sixty-five years. It was not proper to take away the property from his progeny who had not been responsible for the pain and misery Sadanand

and his siblings had suffered. It will be no less a crime than which their forefathers had committed. Sadananda's family will incur the ill will of innocent people which she feared, would fill the lives of her own children with similar bitterness.

' We could have bought many acres of land with the large sum of money we are squandering away in the court case for the mere four acres they have taken away from you in some distant past,' she argued. 'Why are you so bent upon recovering just *those* four acres?'

'Women, and their stupid logic!' Sadanand thought distastefully.

Sumitra never understood that it was not a question of recovering the four acres of land. It was a challenge! It was the question of re-establishing his rightful ownership over the ancestral property! It was an issue of recovering his honour! Sumitra was worried that their tears of frustration and their curse would bring hard luck to her own family because she had no idea how those uncles had blighted the lives of Sadananda and his innocent brother and sister. It was for them Sadananda had to live the life of an exile at Calcutta, toiling hard to support his brother and young widowed sister. It was because of them his brother could not go to school and his sister was forced to take her own life! It was for them that they had been rendered homeless. How could Sumitra realise that that the orphaned Sadananda and his siblings had not wept tears, they had wept blood all those years.

Sadananda went inside. Sumitra sat by the cutting board in the same posture, fidgeting with the vegetables, her face blank.

'Sumitra!''Sumitra!'a voice called tenderly. It was

his own voice, a voice Sadananda felt was coming from within him.

There was no response. No reaction absolutely.

'What sort of a woman Sumitra is?' Sadananda thought bitterly. 'Which wife could remain so indifferent to the victory her husband achieves after years- long suffering and struggle? Which wife would not want to share the joy of that glorious moment with her husband?

But there was no sign of joy or pride on Sumitra's face. Sadananda was getting impatient.

He walked closer and stood before her. Sumitra did not raise her face to look at her husband.

'Sumitra,' Sadanand called softly. Sumitra did not respond and kept cutting the vegetables.

'Are you not happy today? This is the day of our victory.'

Sumitra looked up.

'Yes, we have won', she said looking into Sadananda's eyes. 'It is the triumph of truth and justice. It is the victory of human values. Everyone has realised that. I also know that this victory, for you, is the greatest achievement of your life. Have you ever thought that by snatching away something that had remained in the possession of another for years and years might give a blighted future to our children? Has it ever occurred to you that their tears of misery might cast an evil shadow over our peaceful life? And why should we opt for such a cursed life?'

'Don't you honestly feel,' Sumitra resumed after a heavy, meaningful pause, 'that with all the money we have spent on the court case for winning back our four acres of land could have been used for buying many such plots of land? Couldn't all that money and the precious time you have wasted to vindicate *your* truth have gained us a much better, happy and meaningful life? All the efforts that have been put into a vain pursuit could have been directed to accomplish some other nobler goal.

I know I am an ordinary, brainless woman. But the truth is I am more afraid of this win than happy at it. To me it is more a defeat than a victory. The scene and the sound frighten me! ' Sumitra said darkly and breathed out a deep sigh.

Sadanand stood still and wordless, the glow of joy fading slowly away from his eyes.

The procession had crossed past their house. The rhythmic sound of the drumbeat too was fading away into the distance.

••

The Face of Yesterday

The soft beep from the cell phone startled Suman. She turned her eyes from the computer screen to look at the time. The wall clock showed twenty three minutes past one A.M.

Who could be texting her on line at this odd hour of night? A mixed feeling of doubt and wonder crossed her mind. She picked up the device and looked into the screen.

'How are you?' the message was in Odia language but the alphabets were English. Whoever the fellow may be, Suman guessed, he knew Odia.

Suman was sitting at the computer, browsing data for her children's school project. Her husband Mahesh and her two children had gone to sleep long back.

It was Suman's habit to sit at the computer late into the night. Her husband often warned her that such waking nights would take toll on her health. But Suman found the calm noiseless hours of night most appropriate for concentrating on things. The quietude suited her for doing her children's homework, studying books and writing. That was the time, which was exclusively her own. When there was nothing to do she just sat dozing in the chair keeping the table lamp switched on. Sometimes, in those undisturbed, pensive hours a line of a poem she was contemplating or a plot of a story sneaked into her mind.

She had already downloaded the pictures of different species of animals that lived in deserts, cold regions, and forests. She would need them for preparing her daughter Magna's school project. She would go to a cyber café tomorrow to get the coloured print outs of those pictures. She sat, her eyes glued to the screen searching the period of the Mughal Rule in India. Manav, her son would need the specific details of the Mughal emperors, the tenure of their reign and the wars they fought, the architectural skills displayed in the monuments built during their period, the cultural environment that prevailed then and its distinctiveness, and things like that for his history project. Suman knew that her son did not have much inclination towards history. He was rather more drawn to geography and science. He sat for hours burying his head in the pages of encyclopaedias, watched geographic channels on the television and spent quite a significant portion of his spare time searching , god knows what, from Google. He aimed at becoming a scientist in future.

Her daughter Magna's interest was way apart from her brother. She had a passion for music and art. She craved to listen to songs. She loved to paint and constantly kept humming under her breath. Her husband did not appreciate Magana's obsession with music, but Suman ignored it. Nor did she keep leeched to her daughter and goaded her to pour into her books. She was a kid of seven after all, Suman thought. She would understand things as she grew up in age. Why ruin her childhood exercising pressure on her? Suman wanted Magna to enjoy a long span of childhood.

Another beep from her mobile jerked her out of her thought.

Another online message!

'Hope you are fine!' the message said.

Who could be on line at this time of night, Suman wondered, now considerably disturbed.

And not only that, the fellow had the impertinence to chat with a woman at this time! It was the height of impropriety, she thought angrily. She put the phone on silent mode now, afraid that the distinct beeps might disturb the sleep of her husband and children. The time was half past one. She was beginning to feel a little uneasy. She went to the online site to discover that the fellow was still on line. The time was half past one. She shut the system down. She stopped as her hand reached out to switch off the Wi Fi connection. Curiosity was getting over her uneasiness now. Who could be the person, she was anxious to know more about him. The fellow was not in her contact list. She clicked the display picture of the sender of the message. There was a picture of a desert instead of a photo in the DP. Suman zoomed the picture and squinted again. What sort of a person displays the picture of a desert in the profile? Must be an unemotional, rude character, like the desert! But the picture made her even more curious. She seriously wanted to know more about this mysterious message- sender. She wondered how he got hold of her contact number. It was not difficult though, Suman reasoned out next moment. She was a writer and other writers had her number. Most of her readers had her contact number too. Whenever her articles or stories are published her contact number was given under the article. May be he had collected her number from some such source and was misusing it.

'Why don't you respond?' The next texting flashed on the screen.

For one second she was tempted to retaliate. But, she

pleaded with herself in the next moment, answering back might encourage the fellow to send more messages. She was in two minds. The night was growing dense and deep. Suman's anger and anxiety were growing proportionately.

What an outrageous manner!! Suman fumed within. She switched the phone off and got into the bed. But sleep eluded her. She turned on her sides, desperately trying to sleep. She got off the bed, drank some water, went to the washroom and again got back to bed. Sleep was still miles away from her eyes! 'What do you think you are doing, keeping awake so late into the night?' her husband grumbled drowsily. 'Your blood pressure is rising because you are not getting sufficient sleep. Sleeplessness is causing you acidity and migraine. I have told you several times, but you won't listen to me.

Suman ignored it. Her mind was elsewhere. Her total attention was focused on the mobile and its online message box.

Why would someone text her at such a late hour? Couldn't he find time for that during day time? And the way of inquiring about her was so informal! Why was he kept awake till so late in the night? Questions, questions, questions!! Suman was caught in a web of unanswered questions that threatened to choke her. She turned on her side again and switched on the phone very cautiously. The list of three more messages flashed on the screen.Oh my God! The man was still online. She clicked the app icon and looked.

'I knew you would not respond!'

'I am used to your unresponsiveness!'

'I wish you all happiness!'

Suman's heart skipped a beat. Who could this person be? Only someone very close could write things like this. He must have been someone who knew Suman well. But who? Suman, groped into her memory anxiously to discover a clue to help her identify the person.

She was in a fix. Should she shoot a warning back to the fellow asking him to behave? Or should she first ask him who he was?

She began to type a message and then deleted it. Her heart racing, she typed another message, and again deleted. She could not gather courage to write a reply. The man was still online. He must have noticed her typing and was waiting. No! She made up her mind. She would not write back anything. No decent people chat at this is time of the night.

The man was still there, on line.

Suman tried to calm her anxiety. 'Let him be. Why must I be eager to know about him? He might be one of those lousy flirts who never let go of an opportunity to harass a woman once they got her contact number.

But who was it I have not responded to? How did he know I usually keep silent when asked personal questions?' Despite all her efforts to repress her curiosity the questions crept stubbornly back. She reached for the button to switch of the phone and stopped abruptly. Another message flashed on the screen.

'Why are you awake till now? Trust me , I did not want to disturb you nor did I ever want even in the past. I know I do not deserve your forgiveness now. In fact I did not deserve it then, too. I do not know why you are coming back to my memory, again and again. That is the reason I sent the message. I apologise for disturbing you!'

A gust of sigh heaved out and suffocated Suman.

Siddharth! Yes, this must be Siddharth!

The name came to her like a sudden flash of lightening.

And the face of yesterday flashed on the screen of her mobile phone.

Her heart began to hammer erratically. Her body trembled with an unidentifiable emotion. She found it difficult to breathe, and sat resting her back against the headboard of the bed.

Sidhharth! After so many years!!

As far as she could remember he had left India for good after both his parents died in a car crash. He was their only son. Suman had learnt about the mishap in Siddharth's life and his decision to live abroad from his cousin Madhu who was Suman's classmate. Though she lived in Germany with her husband, Suman was still in touch with her. Madhu had told her that Sidhharth was a professor in some university in US. He had married an American girl and had obtained American citizenship.

Where did Siddahrth get Suman's number? From Madhu most probably, Suman guessed.

And it had to be Siddharth, Suman was sure about that. No one else would dare connect to her on line at this time, nor could anyone be so personal in his approach.

'Here in India it is long after midnight. What must be the time at America now?' She put questions to herself and answered them too. 'Why should Siddharth inquire about her wellbeing after such a long time? 'It must be about twenty two years since they had met last, Suman tried to recollect. It had been twenty years since she had married. But time and again she experienced a mild burning in that twenty year old wound as if it was still fresh. It filled her with a blank gloom.

She remembered the sun scorched noon of May when she had met him last. Sunlight was dropping from the sky as sparks of fire. The heat scalded her body. But Suman's heart was even more scalded than her body was. They sat together smothered under a long, heavy silence. It was Siddharth who broke the silence at last.

'Our horoscopes do not match. My mother is against this marriage. The most important hurdle is the age factor. You are eleven days older than me. In our family the bride must never be older in age than the groom, not even a day. Our marriage is not possible Suman,' Siddharth said brokenly.

It was like a hard slap on the face. Suman felt devastated. It was as if Suman's unflinching trust in Siddharth was suddenly flung into leaping flames of frustration and her years old love for him was burnt to a piece of charcoal.

Her heart broke. The shock and the despair that followed made her wilt. Her mind was not that hard-moulded at that age to absorb the pain. She felt pathetically defeated by life, by time and by love! Siddhartha had left her without saying another word. Nor could Suman gather her confidence that was fast seeping out from her to call him back.

That was the last time she had seen Siddhartha. Years had dragged on. She had married the person her parents had chosen for her and spent an apparently happy life with her two children.

Happy?

Was she really happy ,Suman asked herself sceptically.

Didn't the fire-trail of frustration she had experienced years ago still curl and twist inside her, eating into her carefully maintained complacence? She had tried to think of her meeting with Siddharth like a disastrous accident and made all efforts to fling the intimate memory of the days they spent together far away from her present. But the memory was like a blister that never healed. Several times she thought that the wound had healed and took the shell off despite the pain it caused. But every time she did that the wound had looked fresh and ugly under the shell. The sight had frightened her. She wondered what Siddharth had taken her for, a stuffed toy to play with or some other dispensable object he could get rid of anytime he wanted. She had been brutally deceived in love.

There is no point in brooding over the things gone, she tried to think practically. Once again she turned on her side. But why did Siddharth remember her after all these years, and that too at such a time? She began to feel apprehensive.

Her husband Mahesh asked her many times why her writings reflected so much aversion against men.

'Why does your writing hold such grudging hatred for the male? Do you think all men in this world are images of evil? Do you think all men are savage, oppressors and opportunists? Do all men crave a woman's flesh?'

Suman's reply to her husband was a small smile. She knew there was not any other answer to such questions. 'May be not all men are like that,' she told herself, 'but there are definitely some who disgrace human values. They are the black spots on the face of the society. It is for them the women live an oppressed life, are brutally mauled and mangled. It is they who deny a woman her security and her freedom. My writing is a rebellion against those selfish escapists.'

'Do you see how aggressive your mother is against us men?' Her husband said to their son, Manav, a mischievous smile playing on his face.

Suman failed to make him understand that all men do not come under that category. Most men she had come across were real gentlemen with decent and civil manners. But the presence of a handful of those unscrupulous characters like a few drops of venom in a full pot of ambrosia poisoned the society. Their selfishness and perversion make a woman's life a living hell. Her restlessness gave way to anger. The blood in Suman's veins began to flow in a hot rush. Did Siddharth seek the permission of his parents when he had fallen in love with her? Had he ever inquired about how old was she, by the years, months, and days at that time? How could he behave in such a cowardly manner? And with what face he was sending messages to her after so long a time? What did he want to know? What else is there left in life except pain and torment after love changes to penitence, after commitment becomes a question mark, and promises turn fugitives? Suman felt she was broken into many pieces within, into many personae. One of them sobbed hard, another swallowed a sigh and still another looked vaguely at nothing wearing a withered look.

She realised that the mobile phone was still in her grip. It was switched off though. She would not switch it on, she thought.

'But why? Why shouldn't she turn on the switch of the phone?' Suman thought defiantly. Did she fear Siddharth? Did she still value his reactions and responses? Was he still a priority in her life as he used to be? Why then she was trying to run away from him or from his messages?

Suman switched on the mobile phone.

There was another message!

'I have really been transformed to a desert!' The message said. 'I am nothing but miles and miles of emptiness. Life has become a mirage and I am an unquenchable thirst.

Wherever I turn my gaze I see a measureless void....I see only an emptiness that has no end.'

The storm that had raged in Suman's heart a few hours before had not calmed yet. But she tried to hold her erratic emotions under control. She got down the bed and drank another glass of water. She was sure now that the strange message-sender was none else than Siddharth. She thought that she could now have a peaceful, undisturbed sleep. There was no meaning in lamenting the yesterdays. Why must she reminisce a past that had snatched her dreams away from her eyes, and taught her to abhor love? She tried to shove the bitter memories out of her mind and go to sleep. 'Tomorrow would be a busy day for her. She would have to get up early in morning to ready her children for school. She would prepare breakfast for them and her husband. She would have to cook the main meal and make the lunchboxes ready for them. There were other jobs she would have to attend to like paying the electricity bill at the office since tomorrow was the last date, and go to the bank, go to a cyber cafe and get the printouts of the pictures she had downloaded from the net for her daughter's school project. She would also have to buy books for her son. The list was long enough to keep her on her feet most part of the day working like a machine. Then there were the routine domestic chores, like preparing some light snacks for the evening for her children and her husband, helping the kids in their homework and cooking the dinner. She would have to cater to every need of her family and serve herself out as different dishes to please them.

Suman tried to sleep. It was half past two in the night. Only another two and a half hour left before it was morning. She closed her eyes and then abruptly opened them. The messages were still on her online site. Even though she did not intend to do so she might be tempted to take a look at them and in that unguarded moment Siddharth might once again steal into her thoughts. It would be wise to erase the face of yesterday from the screen of her phone. It was of no use to store the messages of someone who had moved far out of the ambit of her life.

She sat up on bed and deleted the messages one after another.

She recalled her nephew once mentioning about an option every smart phone had for blocking the messages from unknown or unwanted people.

'Notorious characters often trouble people by making false calls or sending disturbing messages once they get hold of their phone numbers. There is an option in the phone to block them,' her nephew had said.

Suman found out the blocking option in her own phone and just as she was about to click it, stopped. Before blocking the man on her phone she had years ago blocked out of her life, Suman's eyes caught sight of the last message he had sent.

'Wish you a happy midnight' it said.

●●

The Song of The Slaughter House

Karim Mian turned back to take a look at the four goats tethered to a post trying to select which one of them he would select as his next victim. Two of the four animals were black, one was a grayish- brown and the healthiest looking among the four was the one with a skin spotted with white. He unknotted the rope at the goat's neck and pulled it inside. The animal began to bleat loudly in utter panic. The other three too, following it started a chorus of hysteric whining.

'Is it male or female?'

' It looks so plump. How much water you have pushed down into it?'

The customers had their questions and their doubts ready for the butcher. But Karim Mian was an experienced man in this trade. He smiled and spat out red betel juice to the road by the side of his slaughter house.

'It is pure *khasi* (castrated male goat). You can check for yourself,' he said convincingly beaming in pride. 'No one can find fault with the stuff I sell. I will not compromise with the rate nor with the quality!'

'Quality indeed!!', one of the men jeered. 'Are you people to be trusted ever? You have your own tricks. No one can even guess when and how you put water into the goat's body to increase the weight of the meat!'

Karim Mian's temper was rising. His anger showed itself in his grim eyes. but he held it in check and tried to speak gently.

'Look, brother. You can take it or leave it. But you must not say such things.'

The crowd in the front of the meat-shop was growing in size. Some motor bikes and cars too had pulled to a stop on the other side of the road.

Karim Mian, in the meantime, had flayed the carcass of the new goat and had hung it from a hook.

His hands busily chopping the meat Karim Mian hummed a song from a Hindi movie

Tum itna jo muskura rahe ho

Kya gham hai jis ko chhupaa rahe ho

(what is that sorrow you are concealing behind your smiles)

Strange!!

A man chopping meat from a goat he had freshly butchered, his body emitting the repulsive smell of flesh and blood , singing melodiously in a voice steeped with such intent sadness!!

Does a butcher have a feeling heart like ordinary human beings? I thought.

'Here, take these. Put them in a polythene packet. Why are you standing there like a statue? How are you going to get your fill unless you work?' He said to the boy that stood leaning to a post. The boy wore dirty knickers that were torn at places, and an equally grubby shirt. A shock of wiry dry hair covered his little head. There was no luster in the eyes that were sunken deep into their sockets. He looked like he was dragged to the place. He had neither any interest nor involvement in the work. It was his fear of his father that forced him to remain stuck to the place.

Karim Mian repeated the lines, and I again wondered how could a man that slaughtered animals, sing a song with so much emotion.

'Babu, the meat is packed for you. I have put a few extra pieces of the goat's liver, for your son.

'Hmm!' One of the customers remarked. 'He could afford to give extra pieces of liver to his favourite customers, but refuse us when we ask him for a few pieces of liver!'

Karim Mian did not react to that. He was busy in weighing meat in the scales for some other customer.

This is how my Sundays used to begin, at the slaughter house of Karim Mian.

He chose the best goat from the lot and always gave me the quality meat. On most of the Sundays the menu in our home is either mutton biryani, pulao with mushily cooked mutton without gravy, or cooked parboiled rice with meat in gravy.

Most of the Sundays I visited Karim Mian's meat shop. I stood waiting, while he chopped the meat for me humming the same song under his breath.

But it is not that I visited Karim Mian's shed only on Sundays. There were other days like the Wednesdays, Fridays when non-veg items were cooked in our home. This of course is a pre conditioned luxury. Bringing non veg to the house was strictly forbidden if it was a day on which some special worship was to be performed. I cannot understand why the ladies impose such restrictions on food.

While returning after leaving my son at school I usually stop by his shed and got meat, provided non veg cooking was permitted at home on that day. One such day I stopped my car by his shop, more out of an old habit than necessity. I had bought one kilo of tiger prawns and there was no need for mutton. As such, my wife used to warn me not to have red meat more than twice or thrice a month. I suffered from hypertension and a raised blood cholesterol level. But I could not resist the temptation and brought mutton frequently making the excuse that our son was fond of it. My wife, however, never hesitated to taunt me for making this lame excuse.

'Why don't you bring the fresh water fish, minnows or some such stuff? They are good for health.' She would be grumbling while cooking meat in the kitchen. I would pretend as if I could not hear her voice above the sounds of cooking, secretly relishing the aroma, my face hidden behind the pages of the newspaper.

But I never gave up on the habit of either getting mutton in large quantities, or getting reprimanded by my wife.

I slowed the car. Karim Mian strode out of the shop. Three goats tied to a post bleated loudly in a frenzy of fear. One carcass hung from a hook. Perhaps no customer had come till then and so the carcass was not knifed till then.

'Babu', he called out .I was surprised at the urgency in his voice. I rolled the glass of the window down and looked at him.

'Wouldn't you please come in for a minute?'

Perhaps he wanted me to be the first customer since no one else had arrived. But I had already bought the prawns,. I told him that and assured him to buy meat from his shop the next time.

'I have something to tell you,' he said imploringly.

I stopped at the act of rolling up the glass and looked at him inquiringly.

'What is it?'

'My son is critical,' he said in a choked voice. 'He is in

the hospital. He needs blood. But the group is not available anywhere, not even in the blood banks. He has to undergo a blood transfusion procedure every three months. He remains active and healthy for about a couple of months after each transfusion. But slowly he gets dull and weak. He is my only son. He suffers from this disease since his birth. I am a poor man. I cannot afford to be regular in arranging blood for him every three months. Sometimes the gap extends to six or seven months. But this time it has exceeded nine months and the cruelest part of it is that the blood group is not available now. The people at the government hospitals are so overbearing in nature! You have an important status in the society, and you move in the upper circles. Couldn't you exercise a little influence to get a few bottles of blood for my son? It would save his life.'

I was filled with a strange disquietude. I had not expected to hear anything like this. The image of a little boy, his pale, drawn face framed by a shock of oil less coppery hair kept returning to my mind. I remembered the day when he had put all the liver pieces in the polythene pack which contained the meat I had bought.

'They are for the sahib's little son!' he had explained to his father.

I wanted to pull the boy into my lap and kiss him, not just because he had put all the pieces of liver in my pack but because he had done it for my son who he had heard was fond of liver pieces. My heart was heavy with an inexpressible gratitude.

That same boy is battling death in a government hospital! He needed blood to win the battle!!

A few customers have gathered in front of his shop. But Karim Mian stood by my car, his palms joined in abject submission, begging me to get his dying son some blood. 'I am requesting every one, and trying every possible means to get the blood of that group. But all my efforts seemed to have gone in vain.'

A deep sigh that seemed to be tearing at my heart escaped me.

'What is the blood group of your son?' I asked at last. AB Positive. It is not available anywhere at present. They say it is a rare group. It is a question of my son's survival. Curse on me! I am responsible for the condition he is in now. My negligence has sent him down to the road of death.' Karim Mian broke into tears.

I had no words to console him. 'Let me see what can be done,' was the only thing I could say before I drove away.

I drove home absently, my mind in turmoil, trying to remember who among my family members or relatives and acquaintances might have AB+ blood group.

My wife was waiting impatiently for me.

'Your boss was trying to reach you. But your cell phone no. was outside network. So he had called on our landline. It must be urgent, because he had called two times. You will have to leave for Bangalore today to attend a meeting. Speak to him immediately.' She said as soon as I stepped inside.

Instantly all thoughts about Karim Mian, his son in the hospital, the rare blood group disappeared from my mind and the face of my dictator General Manager, Mr. Chaturvedi, drifted in. He was a difficult man to be convinced, a real disciplinarian. Without wasting a minute I called him. He answered immediately as if he was waiting for my call.

'Mr Anil, you have to leave for Bangalore today. Actually I was to attend the meeting there but it won't be possible since I have to attend another meeting at Mumbai. Hope you will handle everything there. You will have to make a stop at our Delhi office on your way back. Atul Das has already taken care of your flight tickets and booked the hotel rooms.'

It was already 12 at noon. I had only four hours with me to collect the necessary papers and files and do the packing for a week's stay out. I got busy with making preparations for the journey.

I returned after spending a hectic week at Bangalore and Delhi.

Karim Mian and his son had gone out of my mind. I would not have remembered them had my wife not asked me on that Sunday to get mutton. Her elder sister would be coming to visit us that day along with her family. The mention of mutton suddenly brought Karim Mian back to my mind. I began to wonder what might have happened to Karim Mian's son in the meantime.

I took out the car and drove towards Karim Mian's shop. But the shop was closed. Karim Mian was not there. Fish vendors sat in a row in front of the shop. I inquired from Rahim, Karim Mian's younger brother who sold chicken in the adjacent shed, the reason why the shop had remained closed. Rahim told me that Karim Mian had gone to his village. His son had died in the hospital.

Something broke inside me with a loud clang. As if huge, giant waves rushed wildly one after another from a raging sea and crashed furiously on the shore. It felt as if everything inside me was blighted by a bolt of lightning. As if I was caught in the devastating whirls of a tornado.

The blood transfusion was delayed. Karim Bhai probably had not counted on the disastrous consequences. His delay had caused the problem. Karim Bhai could not arrange the blood of that rare group at short notice and the boy died.

I had nothing more to ask, nothing more to say.

I bought mutton from another shop and returned home.

'Is it quality meat?' My wife asked as she took the polythene pack from my hand. 'My sister's children, like our son, are fond of the liver pieces.' She added and went into the kitchen. I did not want to say anything to her about Karim Mian and spoil her mood. It was she who started the topic.

'This meat is not good. perhaps he had given you the meat of an old female goat. Karim Mian has cheated you today.' She complained while sautéing the meat in the cooker.

It was getting difficult to listen anything against Karim Mian. 'I have not bought it from him,' I broke in before my wife could make any further accusation against Karim. 'His shop is closed today.'

'Why?' My wife asked casually. 'Has he gone to his village? He is a strange fellow indeed. He would be listening to the radio , and humming at the same time while chopping meat. His day won't be made unless it started with listening a song of Mohammad Rafi or Kishore Kumar, she said. What a luxurious way to begin the day! Mad fellow!' My wife said.

I got up from the armchair I was sitting in and walked into the kitchen. My wife was sautéing the meat with the spices with expert hands. The aroma of meat cooking swept through the house. 'His ten year old son had died of thalasemia. The routine blood transfusion he was undergoing was delayed , may be due to lack of money. At the last moment Karim Mian had made all possible efforts to get the rare AB+ blood, but it was of no avail. The boy succumbed to the disease.' I said slowly.

My wife's deft hands sautéing the meat stopped short. 'I had no idea of that…' she said guardedly turning to look at me.

'How could you have? I also came to know of his tragedy just this morning.' I said and went on to narrate how he had requested me to somehow arrange a bottle of this rare blood, and how it had gone out of my mind.

Life moves on following a regular pattern, without waiting for anything or anybody.

Days keep rising in the crimson east, mature and then roll into the pages of history. Time, for me too moved on in a similar manner.

I had visited Karim Mian's slaughter shed more than once during the fortnight that followed the Sunday on which I learnt about the mishap that befell him. I was waiting for him to come back, to share his grief and balm his wound with my sympathy. My failure to arrange the blood, which I probably could have done with some effort and influence but for my lack of concern and my indifference, kept on scraping at my conscience like the blade of a serrated knife.

A month passed. Karim Mian did not return. Rahim told that the death of his only son had affected his mind. His son was his life, Rahim told. It was for his son only he had opted to enter this business of selling meat. He had not the least interest in slaughtering animals. He would have preferred to continue at his job in the bakery had it not been for his son. Whatever he earned working at the bakery was not enough to meet the medical expenses of his son. So he moved in here and set up this slaughter house. Time and again he was asking his customers about their blood group. People had begun to think that he had some mental problem.

Rahim had in the meantime started to sell both meat and chicken. He was afraid that unless he put his brother's shop to use someone might take it over. He wanted to keep the shop in shape and running till his brother returned. It was more the curiosity to know about Karim than the need to get quality meat that compelled me to visit Rahim's shop now and then.

But Karim Mian did not return.

'My brother is born under evil stars. His suffering did not end with the loss of his only son. Much before it his wife had eloped with some vendor leaving this son and a daughter with their father.

'What exactly had happened?' I asked Rahim, anxious to know more about Karim's life.

'His wife had a secret affair with a Sikh fellow. He was a vendor and moved from house to house selling garments. My brother's wife ran away to Punjab with that man. She did not even for once think of her ailing son and little daughter.

That woman had her eyes only on my brother's earning. She was always nagging at my brother; always complaining and grumbling. She did not take care of her son and rather called the boy as her punishment. She cursed her fate constantly for giving her a life which was no less than a hell. She was too proud of her looks. My poor brother tolerated all her taunts and tantrums without a word. He wanted to earn more to keep her happy and for better treatment of his son. So he came to the city and set up this business of selling meat. My brother's absence from home gave her more freedom to maintain a more intimate relationship with that vendor. And finally she left home with him. she might have gone to Punjab. Some said that she was in Hariyana while others said she had gone to either Rajasthan or Kashmir. We are poor people .We do not have enough resource to squander money on a wild goose chase. In the last three years we have had no news of her.

Brother could have married again. But he refused. He was apprehensive that the new wife would neglect his son. "If his own mother deserted him in this condition, what concern would another woman have for him?" That is what my brother said. That woman had broken my brother's heart. Allah will never forgive her!' Rahim sighed.

The death of Karim's little son and the episode of his wife jilting him at the hour he most needed her, had upset me terribly.

'Where is his daughter now?' I asked, unable to suppress my anxiety.

'She died in an accident. She was playing outside her home. No one saw when she had walked towards the village pond. She got drowned.'

Karim was not my friend. He was not my kin too. But a cosmic bond that ties two human beings together had held us close. We shared a relationship which did not have either a name or a definition, or even a future. The strands of some untold but common woe had held our souls tied in a single knot.

Karim had never held out to me the sketch of his unhappy life. He had never told me about the infidelity of his wife, the chronic disease his son suffered from, nor about his daughter's death.

Only when he hummed the song while he chopped meat with deft hands, I wondered how a butcher could have so much emotion within him that prompted him to sing such a song with so much feeling. Was there some secret sorrow that he struggled to conceal under his effusive smiles and jubilant voice?

The echoes of the song that Karim Mian hummed kept coming back to me time and again, when I would be returning leaving my son at his school or while I would be reading the newspaper over my morning tea. Sometimes it rang through the tranquil hours of the nights and I woke up with a start.

I was amazed at the forbearance of Karim Mian, at his art of keeping his calm when the currents of life mercilessly tossed him about in all possible directions.

With each passing day my thoughts were getting more and more possessed by Karim.

On one Sunday when I pulled up at Rahim's shop I saw Karim standing by his brother in the slaughter-shed. He was not chopping meat but only putting them in polythene packets for different customers. I got down and walked up to him. He joined his palms in a polite greeting and smiled a ghost of a smile. 'Hope you are fine, babu!' he said. I was not sure what should I say in reply. What must one say in such a situation, What words of sympathy he must use to console the person who he knew was beyond all consolation?

I swallowed hard. 'How are you Karim? I haven't seen you for a long time.' I managed to say with much effort.

He smiled again, the same zombie smile. 'I am alright babu. Just dying every day in small, small installments.

The reply gave me a jolt. He did not say a word about his son. But how precisely and how clearly he explained the truth of his life!

I did not have the heart to ask him about his son. Nor

could I summon the courage to explain to him how despite my concern I could not do anything for his son on account of my urgent official commitments. Sympathy or explanations were just empty words for him and for me too, now.

For the next two Sundays I did not go to the meat shop of Karim to get mutton because my distantly related uncle had died and we were in mourning. On the Wednesday when I reached at my son's school, I learnt that the school would remain closed on that day because of the sudden demise of the chairman of the board of directors of the school. That was unexpected and I had to return home bringing my son back. I decided that I would get some mutton from Karim's shop on my way back. I had not met Karim for near about two weeks and I was prodded with an anxiety to see how he was doing.

I found both the brothers busy in chopping and packing the meat for the customers. Most of the good meat on the carcass that was hanging was sold away and I stood waiting there for Karim to slaughter another goat. My son stood beside me.

'Shouldn't you keep some clean water in the shop to wash your hands?' One of the customers remarked. Karim came out of the shop, a bucket in hand and walked to the tube well on the other side of the wide road to get fresh water. I had no idea when my son had run right to the middle of the road chasing a puppy. Karim Mian was returning with the bucket of water. he was the first to notice the truck that was speeding towards my son.

Everything seemed to have happened almost at one time. Karim Mian flinging away the bucket of water and rushing towards my son, and pushing him away to the other side where I stood, and the truck hitting him. My heart skipped a few beatings and I closed my eyes.

When I opened them I found my son clutching at me and trembling all over. I tried to look through the jostling crowd. Karim's lay on the road, his body reduced to torn limbs and scattered pulps of blood and flesh.

The body of the butcher lay in bloody pieces just in front of his own butchery. The heat of the freshly butchered body began to run down my veins, crippling my thoughts. A few drops of tears trickled down my eyes as my son held my hand in a fearful grip. I stood there rooted to the ground, the realization slowly creeping into me that my guilt now has become my eternity.

There was nothing between Karim Mian and me that could have been called a definable relationship except for the one of the salesman and the customer. Neither was our relationship conditioned by any commitment towards each other, nor did it hold any promise for the future.

Did the guilt and remorse snowballing inside me mirror the ever growing shadows of those bloody pulps of flesh?

The question tore me apart, shattered me. It ruined me.

●●

White Crow

They say predawn dreams often come true.

She had never had an opportunity to verify it.

Dreams rarely visited her sleep.

They always changed path before they found a way into her disturbed sleeps. She wondered if at all the few discordant, disjointed flashes that drifted into her sleep could actually be called dreams. Because they were just a disorganised collage of random scenes without any pattern or order. She never remembered them.

Truth be told, she had never had experienced the luxury of a sound sleep all these years, and hence, dreams always eluded her sleep.

A light, post-lunch nap was something next to impossible.

And it was usually midnight by the time she went to bed at night after wrapping up all the domestic chores. Sleep did not come easily to her. Her mind, cluttered with several house hold issues and planning for the next day, kept sleep at bay for a long time. Sometimes, a few indistinct lines of a poem that had disappeared from her imagination before beginning to take a definable shape stole into her memory. There were even those rare moments when she herself tried to pull out a line from a poem that had tried to come up but had squirmed into a secret corner inside her frightened of the angry frowns of her husband. There are times when the effort of retrieving that line from within tormented her till the night began fading into the dawn.

No sleep, no dreams.

But she dreamt of something very, very unusual that night. It was almost dawn by the time the dream visited her sleep. And it was not a discordant and intriguing pattern, but a clear, organised visual.

It was a visual in a time-future, some forty years later.

She could see a large hall, brilliantly lit. There was a raised platform at one end, and rows of chairs were placed in its front. There were chairs on the dais too, for the dignitaries obviously. It was some kind of a literary meet, she guessed. The next moment she realised that the literary meet was organised for launching her own poem collection and to felicitate her. She could see a large photograph of her in an ornate frame hanging on the wall. It was a photograph snapped a few days after her marriage. In fact it was a joint photo of her and her husband, and the photo on the wall was a cropped and enlarged version of her own. Another such cropped and enlarged photo of her, framed nicely, stood on a side table. It was another joint photograph of she and her husband, she remembered, taken many years after, for attaching on the pension papers of her husband. Both the photos were garlanded. She wondered why, and suddenly, like a lightning flash, it came to her! The event was taking place forty or so years after, and she had died in the mean time!!

There was a big brass lamp-stand in front of her photo. She knew that lighting the lamps was a common ritual before the beginning of such meetings. She could see herself counting the chairs on the dais and making a guess at the number of guests on the dais. She could see herself moving to the last row and cautiously taking a convenient seat close to the exit door from where she could easily come out unobserved from the hall in case she was needed by her family. She always did that, sit in the back row, intending not to disturb the meeting by the ringing of her cell phone. She knew that it would ring, at irregular intervals. The caller could be anybody, her husband, her son, daughter-in-law, her daughters or her grandson.

Her husband would yell at her from the other end-

'Where is that office file I had given you to keep? Why did not you take it out before you left? Come now and get me the file!'

Then her son's impatient voice would come floating in,

Maa! 'Where have you kept my voter ID card and my passport, ma? I can't find them. Come and find them for me... NOW!'

'Ma, I cannot cook this *mahura*(a dish of mashed fish-heads and vegetables cooked in mustard paste)ma,' the daughter in law would complain,

'You have to come and prepare it before it is time for father to take the insulin injection. My son too have to have an early lunch.' The complaint soon took the form of a demand.

Sometimes it was her elder daughter,

'Ma, come here before the examination of my children begins. I and your son in law are taking a trip to Switzerland. You will have to take care of the kids during our absence. A question of just fifteen days...!!'

Or, her younger daughter who was in the family way,

'Ma, you should better come now. I have started developing complicacies. I will be needing you here...'

There were occasions when her school going grandson wanted to know about eminent literary personalities of Odisha from her.

'Who is Sachi Routray, granny? I have to submit a school project on him, a write up on his poem *Chhota Mora Gaan Ti'* (My Village is a Small One). I will also need a photograph of the poet. Why have we been asked to write about Sachi Routray? Is he a great poet?'

She knew she could not ignore any such phone call. She also knew that she lived other people's lives and other people's time. Anyone could invade her private space at any point of time. In fact she had no space of her own. She had always been a taken-for- granted character by all her family members.

They would never care to take note of her wish to attend a literary meeting such as this, much in the same way the audience present in that meeting would care to take note of her presence or absence there.

But, she thought with a sense of relief, nothing of the sort would possibly happen because she was no longer a human of flesh and blood!

Her eyes turned to the activities going on in the hall. She could see her granddaughter busy in supervising the arrangements. It was she who seemed the most active amongst all. She was moving here and there briskly, making the last minute preparations. Her eyes softened as she looked at the young woman. She could very well remember the circumstances in which she was born. It was Deepavali, the festival of light. It was a holiday and no male member was at home when her daughter started to have the labour pain. Finding no alternative she had hired an auto rickshaw to get her daughter to the nearest hospital, but it was too late and the baby was born in the auto rickshaw.

Everyone, including the child's own mother believed her to be evil since she was born on a no-moon day of Deepavali. They thought she would bring ill luck to the family as well as herself. Despite all the neglect and loveless indifference the baby grew up to be beautiful and intelligent girl. And a time came when the very ones that considered her evil, doted on her. But it was she, her grandmother, who loved the girl most. She was, after all, the eldest progeny of the next generation!! The girl was an excellent student, a singer, a dancer, all rolled into one. That was not all though. No one could stand a match to her expertise in swimming and horse riding.

The young girl too was an ardent admirer of her grandmother.

After she passed her school finals her parents sent the girl abroad for higher studies. On the eve of her departure she had come to her grandmother.

'I will read your poems when I become big girl,' she had told the old woman. 'I am not able to grasp much from them now. But I will surely translate them in English when I grow up and bring the poems which you are writing secretly, to light. I will let the whole world know you. I will, in your poetry, meet that invisible lover of yours you have pined for ages, the one for whom you have spent numberless sleepless nights writing poems.

Rivulets of tears streamed down her eyes. 'This little girl, in spite of her tender age has understood what a bitter agony her life has turned to!!'

Separation from her granddaughter had thrown her into an all-devouring emptiness. Each day became an endless waiting, a soul-consuming torment!

But she did not have to live through that agony for long. One day while performing the worship her sari caught fire from the flame of the clay- lamp and soon the fire devoured her, alive.

Had she been alive she would have laid her heart open before her granddaughter after she returned from abroad. She would have narrated to her the torments of her wasted life. She would have told how all her life she had craved in vain for a little love!!

She had lived an apparently fulfilled life with a big family of her husband, six children and many relatives. She had discharged all her familial responsibilities with utmost sincerity and commitment. But she had always remained detached from the mundane life. Material possessions that would supposedly have brought a sense of completeness like it does to most women, failed to do so in her case. And what she had believed to have brought her real bliss and a total fulfilment was despised by the world as wrong and a profanity.

Every moment of her life was a vain search for an indefinable figure of a lover she had conjured up through her fancy.

She often wondered who that loved one was whom she had waited for all her life. He sent a stir through her nerves without being ever in a touching distance. He never came within the range of her vision, but she could sense his presence each and every moment. How could she have described that lover of hers who so filled her dreams, yet did not have a form or a shape?

She was obsessed with a desire to discover him, to be close to him and it was that intense longing that urged her to write poems after poems!

No one understood poetry in her family.

No one appreciated her writing.

Constant repulsion and relentless derogation smothered the breath of the poetry that lived inside her.

She neither protested nor defended, but had never distanced herself from her poetry. All these discouragements had made her to cling to her passion with a silent obstinacy.

Every time she sat down to write a line one or other family member would come up with some kind of a demand. The demand would always be accompanied with a caustic remark on her hobby of poem writing. Her heart became heavy, and the string of imagination that held words, snapped.

She hardly found a brief moment of respite. Her domestic chores kept her busy from morning to evening. She hardly found a brief moment of leisure to jot down the line her mind spun around unceasingly. And the line would get lost in oblivion, forever.

She shed secret tears to lament the loss. It was like losing someone of your own permanently. Unheard sobs wracked her heart. She could not share her sorrow with anyone not even her husband. She knew her people would look down upon her emotions as something ridiculous.

Kandhei (doll), her granddaughter, might have understood her restlessness, she had hoped. But before the girl became matured enough to grasp the sense in her poems, she was sent abroad to pursue higher studies.

The girl has now grown up to a woman now, a wife and a mother. She takes after her grandmother, she thought happily. The same eyes, the same shape of the nose and the same style of articulation!!

She let her gaze sweep around the hall once again. In the first row of seats facing the dais, sat the eminent literary figures of the city. Except for her eldest daughter in law and her second son-in-law all other members of her family were present there.

There were eight chairs on the dais. The invited guests occupied five of them, and in the rest three were seated her granddaughter Kandhei and two of the organisers of the event.

The meeting would begin now. She began rummaging inside her handbag for the mobile phone. Was the phone ringing? Was her husband calling? She thought fearfully.

'Were you sleeping? Your phone has been ringing for such a long time. Can't you hear it?' And then there would flow a stream of abuses from the other end!

But in the next moment she realized that she did not have a body now. It was her spirit that was sitting here as a mute shadow. Nobody could see or hear her, but she heard everyone and saw everything. She breathed a sigh of relief. Her phone would not be ringing anymore now. She could now hear the speeches made by the guests in a calm undisturbed mind.

She saw the guests leaving their chairs and moving towards her photo to light the lamps. They looked glum. Silence hung in the hall. This meeting was organised for felicitating a poet, a woman-poet to be more accurate, posthumously, after twenty five years of her death.

'Why do you remember her so many years after her death?' Someone remarked from the seats in the rear.

'She has not received the honour and lauding she was worth while she was alive!' Someone else returned.

'It is because our literature has not recognised her worth. She was not given the weightage and glory she deserved as an author.

'Her own family has never approved of her writing!!' another voice said.

'She had the heart of a great lover. She had written

piles and piles of love poems but they were never compiled and published as a collection.'

'Her poems were so intense!!' someone else remarked. ' Even if you read them now they can make your hair stand on end!''

'Look at her eyes. How liquid is the gaze!! That gaze is Poetry itself!!'

'A collection of her poems, her Complete Works will be launched in this meeting. ' another voice added.

She could hear everything. Her eyes brimmed in tears. She made an involuntary effort to raise her hands to wipe away the tears that began to trickle down.

But reality dawned on her in the next instant. How could she do that? She did not have hands anymore! Nor eyes! She was body less now!

One after another, the invited guests spoke about her poetic craft, showering laudations on her.

'She could create wonderful poetry in spite of remaining chained to her domesticity.' A renowned poet remarked.

Another one was reciting lines from her poems.

'There was fine a blending of romance and mysticism in her poems. The love she professed in her poems was not for any character of flesh and blood. They are mostly spiritual in nature. Love and prayer were the prominent streaks in her poetry.

'Her poetry reads like contemporary writing,' A relatively younger speaker was saying.

The eldest among the guests, who presided over the meeting spoke about how she had been deprived of the due honour despite her lifelong struggle to create poetry.

The chief guest, cited the instances of the failed marriages of poet Kamala Das and of Amrita Pritam, and narrated how the troublesome domestic life could never hinder their literary pursuit. He also spoke about Padma Sachdev and Habba Khatun, and their literary ventures. These women poets, the guest said, had never given in to the impediments life posed before them. He narrated how boldly Habba Khatun defied her arrogant husband Sultan who had chastised her for writing love poems. After drawing a comparison with them the chief guest lauded her with appreciation. 'It is a wonder how our poet could write thousands and thousands of poems and proved her worth in the teeth of all odds,' he added.

Her lips curled up in an ugly, derisive smile as she heard all those words of praise and admiration as she recalled the bitter agony of her poetry writing days. The world does not know what she had gone through. It does not know the pain of those unbearable humiliations, of her ceaseless battle with the urge of putting an end to her life. She had very carefully kept them hidden inside her.

The convenor of the meeting explained the need of arranging such an event after twenty five years of the death of the poet. 'We are fortunate to have been able to organise such an event,' he was effusive.

Now it was the turn of Kandhei, her granddaughter, her doll!

She stood up and walked to the podium. Kandhei was wearing glasses. She too had grown in age. But she had not put on any weight.

'Kandhei was always choosy about food and never ate anything with relish. That is the reason why she is like this!'

She thought to herself.

Kandhei stood for a while in a stunned silence.

Why? She wondered, and then saw the tears in her granddaughter's eyes.

'Don't weep my precious,' she tried to raise her hands and wipe away Kandhei's tears. But she had no hands!! She heaved out a frustrated sigh.

Kandhei had started speaking .

'My grandmother was a fairy! A real one!!' She was saying.

'She had that strange alchemic touch to transform everything to gold! Her eyes held a blue sparkle. She had a heart that flooded with crystal-white love and compassion.

She was not an ordinary woman, my grandmother! She was not a woman if I am to tell the truth. She was someone like god!!

That was the reason her poems sang of love and prayer and that was why they celebrated resilience!

It is true that she remained detached from the mundane world. But she could salvage new meanings and new promises for life!

Grandmother had her grievances against time, but she smoothly patted them to sleep. She was dispassionate but that dispassion gave her the strength to battle the ignominy the world had afflicted her with. The purpose of this meeting is not to examine what my grandmother has or has not achieved during her life, but to commend her confidence in herself with which she stood up to the adversities to bloom and scatter the scent around!'

'How articulate her granddaughter has become!' She thought with pride and joy. She herself could never have spoken like this in such a gathering. She had never examined or judged her nature or competence in her entire lifetime. Leave that alone, she thought bitterly, she had never had the freedom to speak or even laugh in her own natural way.

But, no! She held nothing against anyone now.

Wasn't it just enough that her granddaughter, if not anyone else, could read her mind and had organised a literary event to commemorate her even after twenty five years of her death!! Wasn't it enough that she could sit through the whole of the meeting without a frisson of fear? May be she was disembodied, but that hardly mattered.

She roamed like a doomed spirit all these years. But finally she was redeemed. She had been relieved of a big responsibility. She would have nothing more to expect from anyone. Nor would her poems accuse her any longer for keeping them veiled and unnoticed from the eyes of the world. Her granddaughter had taken charge of everything. It was now her responsibility to find the right place for her grandmother's poems.

She turned her gaze towards the dais. Her granddaughter climbed down the steps and took her seat at one corner of the hall. Even from that distance she could see Kandhei weeping. Hard sobs wracked her frail body. 'She was like this since she was a child,' her grandmother thought gloomily, 'sentimental!' Staying abroad all these years and getting educated there had not changed her a bit.

'Don't cry my child! Your grandmother is with you!' She felt choked with her own sobs as she tried to speak out the words.

Her complete collection of poems was released. The meeting was formally over. People, one by one were leaving the hall. The invited guests were holding a book each. She tried to see the book but could not get a clear glimpse. She was curious to see the cover page, and the contents too. Which of her poems were listed in the book, she was filled with a strange anxiety now.

She remembered the one which had so preoccupied her mind that she had absently put her hand in the hot oil while frying pakodas. Was that poem included in the collection? Was there the poem there thinking about which she had slipped from the staircase of their three storied house?

While she was in labour during the birth of her first child and was screaming in pain, a few lines of a poem had involuntarily escaped her and immediately after she screamed out those lines her eldest daughter had slid off her womb. She had completed the poem later. Was that poem there in that anthology?

There was never enough time for her to sit at one spot and concentrate on her poems. She recalled the incident when she had to get up to clean the vomits of her son leaving her writing halfway through. Her husband had read the lines she was writing and rushed at her, his face distorted with an ugly snarl. Strangely, she was not scared. Rather she had smiled. His doubt and the anger resulting from it, instead of frightening her, had made the writing of the rest of the lines easier.

Was the poem that had given her sleepless nights in its constant urging to be written down, included in the list? And has the poem that used to make tears stream down her eyes been there amongst others?

She could remember another poem, titled 'The Scent of the Jasmine Garland' and the flaring rage of her husband. He had torn the paper she was writing the poem on into pieces.

There was a poem, which though being in its embryonic stage had got imprinted in her mind. She used to hum the lines under her breath till she could eke out a little time from her busy days to scribble them on a piece of paper.

Then there was that poem on darkness where she

had written how darkness could be charged with a strange sense ecstasy of fulfilment even though the two persons engulfed in it could neither see nor touch each other.

'Are all these poems there in the collection,' she was desperate to know.

If at all she could cast a brief glance at the content of the collection!! She thought wishfully. She looked around and saw her granddaughter was engaged in conversation with a man.He was a famous poet of the contemporary times.

'You have done a great job', he said patting her daughter's back. 'Your grandmother, if she would be watching you from wherever she was, would be so happy at what you have done for her!'

She remembered the man. He was beginning to write poems then. Now he has become a widely acclaimed poet.

She saw people buying the book from the stall. The books were sold at a 50 % discount.

Should she squeeze her way through the crowd to the stall and take a look, she thought unsurely. She would run her hand tenderly on the book just once! She was feeling a little euphoric as she had felt after the birth of her first son.

But, no! The painful realization hit her like a cold blast. It would not be possible now.

Once again rivulets of tears rolled down her eyes. This was a time of joy and fulfilment. She must not cry in such an occasion. She reprimanded herself and tried to smile.

'Grandmother! O, grandmother!!' She heard a voice calling her from somewhere and felt hands nudging at her body. 'Why are you weeping and laughing in your sleep? Is goddess Sathi making you laugh and cry at the same time?'

The voice of a little girl! Yes, it was her five year old granddaughter, Kandhei!

She was jerked out of her sleep and sat up on the bed. Her daughter in law stood by her bed looking worried, her hand resting on the post of the bedstead.

'What is the matter with you Ma? 'She asked in concern. 'You are crying and laughing in your sleep. Have you had a dream or what?' it is already seven o clock. You are in the habit of getting up at four in the morning. So I came to your room to see. I was worried when I saw you laughing and weeping like this! Are you alright, Ma?'

Slowly she came back to herself.

'Grandmother, I saw a white crow in my dream. It sat on the edge of our balcony and cawed nonstop. I woke up and it was dawn. Didn't you say that there was no such thing as a white crow! But I had this dream early in this morning and mother says that predawn dreams come true. Will a white crow actually come to perch on the edge of our balcony?

And what was *your* predawn dream that made you laugh and cry simultaneously? Kandhei asked, a naughty twinkle in her eyes and laughed.

'Yes, I too had a dream…. of something like a white crow!!'

She pulled her five year old granddaughter to her lap and smiled.

●●

The Deal

Every night before he took to bed Debadutta was haunted by a premonition. A terrible fear that he might have been sacked from his post when he reached next morning at the newspaper office where he worked kept him awake late into the night. He would turn restlessly on his sides and would retrospect upon his whole day's work wondering if he had made any involuntary slip, drink several glasses of water and frequent the wash room before drifting into an uneasy sleep. He knew that if he had made even a slightest mistake he would be jolted out of sleep by the shrill ringing of his phone before the daybreak and the moment Debadutta picked up the call there would flow in a hot current of tirade from the other end scalding Debadutt to the very core of his being. The one invariable threat that was never missing from that rush of invective was that of the dismissal from the job. Debadutta had no choice but to listen to the abuses without interrupting. Nor could he afford to disconnect the phone. This happened more than once in a week which turned his morning into another nightmare. In the beginning the humiliation of silently swallowing the abuses of the boss tempted the disconcerted Debadutta to tender resignation from the job but his colleagues dissuaded him from taking such a rash step.

'The old man is a patient of hypertension. He flies into a temper whenever there is a rise in his blood pressure,' Soumendra and Rajiv would remark. We have to put up with such opprobrium if we have to work here. The only way to survive here is to ignore it.'

'That oldie is some sort of a Casanova,' they would add,' and flirts with women of all ages. They say that he has a disturbed family life. His wife is mostly occupied with activities of yoga and pranayama, or visit to the temples and performing religious rituals. The man too had to encounter repeated failures in his political career. He does not show it to others but he is a frustrated character and lives through terrible stress. And he very conveniently takes all this frustration out on us.Aren't we his poor, acquiescent employees? '

For one brief moment Debadutta's heart would go out to the old man as he listened to the views of his colleagues. 'Poor man!!' He would feel something approximating pity for his boss. But the feeling would pass as quickly as it came. 'Bloody tyrant,' he would curse him, 'we hold degrees and certificates that could get us much better jobs. It is our sheer ill luck that compels us to slave here. Why must he hurl such indignities at us as if he is doing some kind of charity by paying us salary?'

He would ask this question to himself every time he received an abusive call early in the morning from his vindictive boss, and would grope vainly for an answer. The sun would be creeping up the eastern sky. He would drag heavy, depressed feet to the balcony and look across the street at the houses to see life awakening slowly to face another busy morning.

The school bus would come and the kids would scramble into it amidst loud chatters. Debadutta would come inside after the bus drove off and make tea.

It was becoming difficult to afford the rent of the relatively large house with the meagre salary the newspaper office paid him. Earlier, he and Subrat, one of his colleagues lived there. They shared the rent and other ancillary expenses between themselves. But Subrat got a transfer to his home district after two months. The transfer, however, was not done in Subrat's interest. The real reason was something else. The place to where Subrat was transferred happened to be the MD's electoral constituency. Since the general election was round the corner, he was sent there to promote public relation and build up news in favour of the MD who contested from the place. Subrat was a shrewd newsperson and could prove effective in conjuring up an agreeable image of the MD through his glib reporting. He was the trusted and reliable newsman of the MD. 'Every journalist must master the craft of manipulating the truth, and learn the art of collecting the buyoff too,' the MD used to point out from time to time.

Debabrata remembered the day Manoj went to the chamber of the MD with a request for a pay hike. His salary had remained stagnant at five thousand a month. With the frequent price rise of different commodities it was getting impossible for him to manage his expenses, Manoj explained, trying to draw the boss's sympathy. The MD had laughed loudly, a raucous, sneering laughter.

'Should I have to teach you the trick of earning extra money? What for do you do the job of a news reporter? The office cannot pay you much. You yourself have to find out the means of earning more using your strategy. Aren't your fellow reporters living a life of luxury with the same salary which the office pays you?It is because they know the trick to pull things off.'

Manoj gaped helplessly at the boss trying to solve the riddle in which he was talking.

'Ask your friends and collect from them the tips for getting easy money. You must not expect me to be more explicit than this.' The MD said with a tone of dismissal and Manoj came out of the room, looking grim and thoughtful. What the MD was suggesting covertly, he understood, was called blackmailing in criminology!!

Aditya gave him a knowing smile as Manoj lowered himself to his chair.

'I knew the oldie would never give a pay hike to us. These are different days, and you would be starved to death with your 'honesty is the best policy' motto,' he said solicitously. 'Look at us! We too had held on to honesty in the beginning of our career, but circumstances compelled us to betray the professional ethics. Hunger gave a sharp twist to the straight and simple life we lived.' Aditya taught Manoj the trick to earn easy money.

'That single news you are working on now, if handled cleverly, would get you enough money to last a year. There won't be any need to touch your salary.'

Manoj looked at Aditya, confused.

'How?'

Aditya laughed at Manoj's innocence. 'What a silly question! It is simple. Approach the minister involved in the scandal your story is going to expose. Put through a call to him and give him a hint about it. The minister will himself find out the means to reach you and he will eagerly pay any amount he was asked to pay for suppressing the news. He had, at this age, got himself entangled with a young girl studying first year in the college. The news will unleash a huge outcry if it gets public. It will send an electrifying stir through the State Assembly. The opposition party will make all efforts to use it as a lethal weapon against the government. The fellow would offer you any amount you bargain for. Accept the buyoff amount and drop the news. You will be instantly rich.'

'I can't do such a thing.'

'Then rot here and let your family rot, too.'

'What will happen if the MD comes to know about it?'

'Our MD is not as clean as he shows himself to be. If you do not exploit that lecherous minister the MD will do it and collect from him an amount ten times more than you could have...'

The mild hiss of tea frothing out of the pot brought Debadutta back to present.

Someone was ringing the doorbell urgently. Who could be visiting him at such early hours, Debadutta wondered. He walked up to the front door and opened it. His father, looking tired and dishevelled stood outside.

Debadutta was surprised at this unexpected and unannounced visit of his father.

'What is the matter, father?' He asked apprehensively.

'Your mother is very ill. The fever is not coming down,' his father said and came inside mopping his face with the *gamchha* that slung from his shoulder.

Debadutta looked at his father. He had perhaps come here by the first bus that starts from his village at early dawn. He looked pale and drawn. In all probability he hadn't had time to eat anything before boarding the bus.

'Would you have tea father? I will get you some snacks from the nearby shop.'

'Do not bother about that. I can manage with some beaten rice,' his father said, sounding impatient.

'Your mother is practically plastered to the bed. I had taken her to the local hospital. The doctor says to get her admitted in a good hospital and get some tests done. A small bit of flesh has to be cut from some part of her body and the sample will have to be sent to Bombay to be tested. I am at my wit's end. What should we do now?'

Debadutta's head began to spin. 'The doctor is advising a biopsy! Does he suspect cancer…? God forbid!! It couldn't be that dreadful,' he tried to control his rising panic and sat down by his father.

'Don't you worry so much, father,' he said consolingly, hiding his fear. 'We shall get all the tests done.' He did not want to show his own anxiety to his father. He was the only son in the family. His elder sister had married and the younger sister Rini, was only eighteen. He was the only hope of his father. He will have to find out a means to deal with this crisis. He had to bring his mother here, get her admitted in a good hospital and get all the tests done. But how? Where will he get the money needed for all this? The question nagged at his mind as he listened to his father.

'Our lands had to remain unfarmed this year. The croft-farmers are bargaining for a three fourth share of the yield. Who would lend them land for farming on such conditions? I have not the strength or drive do the farming myself. The farmhands and the daily-wage labourers come very expensive these days. Besides, there are a pair of cows and another pair of bullocks that need to be looked after. Your mother is too weak to handle the regular domestic chores. Life is getting more and more difficult..' A cloud of gloom hung on his face as father narrated the tale of his suffering.

Debadutta had made up his mind to do whatever possible on his part to help his father. His father had never questioned his expenses and provided everything he required for his studies. He had not hesitated to sale his land to meet the expenses of his son's education. It was now Debadutt's turn to fulfil his duty. After assuring him that he would take the responsibility of mother's treatment, Debadutta saw his father off at the bus stand.

It was past eleven by that time Debadutta reached his office. He headed straight for the account section.

Mishra babu, the accountant, munching *paan,* looked over at him questioningly.

'Sir, namaskar!'

'Namaskar, What brings you here?

'My mother is ill sir,' Debadutta explained. 'I have to get her admitted in a good hospital and get some tests done. It wouldn't be less than a fortnight before the office paid me salary. I need some advance urgently, sir.'

'You can get the tests done next month, after you receive your salary. That will not make a very big impact on your mother's health ,' Mishra babu said unfeelingly.

Debadutta wanted to pull at the collar of the man's shirt and throw him out of the chair. It took him a lot of patience to hold his anger in check.

'My mother is very serious. She needs immediate medical attention,' Debadutta said forcing subordination into his voice.

'But you had already taken an advance of ten thousand a few months ago for your sister's marriage. You have repaid only four thousand out of it. Sorry, I can't help you. You must meet the MD if the need is that urgent. With his say-so I can sanction any advance amount in your favour. But you have to obtain a written permission of the boss for that.'

Debadutta felt a twinge of disappointment as he walked out of the account section.

Naik, the MD'S personal peon sat on a stool by the closed door of his chamber.

'Is the boss in?' Debadutta asked him. 'I want to see him. It is urgent.'

'The boss is busy in an important meeting. Can't your problem wait till after sometime?'

'No. Didn't I tell you it is urgent?'

'You have to wait here, then,' Naik said. 'The boss has categorically asked me not to disturb till the meeting was over.'

Debadutta stood waiting outside the MD's chamber. After about two hours and fifteen minute's the door of the chamber opened and madam Harshita, the wife of the boss's friend, emerged from it smiling slightly through her heavily painted lips. She walked away running her hand through her loosened hair, adjusting her sari over the shoulder.

'So, this was the person the MD was holding an important meeting with!' Debadutta said to himself.

'You can go in now,' Naik said. 'I have given the slip to sir.'

Debadutta pushed the door and entered.

'Namaskar, sir!' He said and walked towards the MD's table.

The boss did not response to that. He went on leafing through the pages of a file, with apparent concentration.

'Why do you want to see me? What is the urgency?' he asked Debadutta a little irritably without raising his eyes from the file.

'Sir, my mother is seriously ill. It has been nearly a month she is suffering from fever,' Debadutta said politely.

'Oh! You want leave of absence once again! Haven't had you availed leave of absence last month?'

'It is not leave of absence sir,' Debadutta explained.

'Not leave of absence? What do you want then?' The boss raised his eyes from the pages of the book and looked at him questioningly.

'I need some advance amount sir.'

'Oh! So, you need money!' the MD scoffed. 'Doesn't the office pay you salary every month? What do you need an advance payment for?'

'Salary!!'Debadutta thought sourly. Four thousand and five hundred rupees!! . ' After meeting all the regular expenses and with nil saving, the little amount left with him was not enough to get him a frugal meal a day during the entire month.

'What are you thinking?' the MD asked. 'Have you repaid the loan you have taken for your sister's marriage?'

'No sir, there is another six thousand rupees to be paid,' Debadutta replied meekly.

'How could you be given a fresh advance amount unless you clear the backlog? How can I run this establishment if I go on squandering money in this manner? You are a sensible person. Do I have to explain it to you?'

'I know sir. But my mother is serious...'

'It is just a fever,' the boss broke in. 'Why do you sound so alarmed as if she is in her last stage? The treatment can wait till you get the salary for this month. Now you must leave. I have a lot of important engagements,' the MD said dismissively and returned his gaze to the pages of the file.

Debadutta came out of the chamber, feeling utterly helpless. He had lost his appetite and instead of going for lunch he came to the staff common room and sat down in front of the desktop. He opened the system and logging in to the internet began browsing through the list of medical tests required to be done for the diagnosis of the dreaded disease.

'Is it cancer..?' he asked himself again and again, his mind obstinately refusing to accept the possibilities. He knew that there was no permanent cure for the disease. One of his uncle and one aunt had succumbed to cancer only a month after it was detected.

'Oh God! Please help us! Let it be some ordinary fever. Let it not be cancer. It will shatter our family!' he begged of god desperately. He shut the system down and went to the office. He was pleasantly surprised to find Swapnajit there. Swapnajit worked for another news establishment. He was a moneyed man. He lived a luxurious life and spent lavishly.

'Would it be proper ask for a loan to Swapnajit? After all he was rich and a good friend too. How would Swapnajit take it? Will he agree to lend him the money or turn his request down? He may or may not agree, but there is no harm in trying,' Debadutta wrestled with his conscience before giving in to his helplessness. He explained to Swapnajit the terrible plight he was in before making the request. Surprising Debadutta, Swapnajit took five thousand rupees out of his wallet and handed it to him without asking a question. 'Don't you worry at all to pay it back in a hurry. Return it at your own convenience. Let your mother be cured first.' Debadutta's eyes brimmed with tears of gratitude. God had filled the world with people of diverse kinds of mentality. There was the MD who was so rude and apathetic and here was a friend who came like a godsend to help him out of his worries!!

His mother's health was deteriorating by the day. Debadutta got her admitted in a hospital at Bhubaneswar. Debadutta's worst apprehensions proved to be true. His mother was diagnosed with cancer. The sky as though came crashing down on Debadutta's head. The chemotherapy was to be done immediately and that required quite a large amount of money. There were several other expenses including the medicines, blood transfusion and many other medical procedures. Debadutta borrowed money from some of his relatives but that was not enough. The treatment cost a lot more than he could arrange from all possible sources.

Despite his unwillingness he had to approach the boss once again.

'The sickness of your mother is your problem,' the MD said after Debadutta told him about his mother's condition. 'I can't help you. You know that this establishment is running in loss. I have spent a large amount of money from the exigency fund of the office for contesting the election. I had hoped to return the money to the office fund after winning the election. But fate was not in my favour. How can I extend any financial support to you when I myself am not sure how to reimburse the amount I have borrowed from the office fund? You have to handle your problem yourself.'

Debadutta felt like spitting at the boss's face. How could a human being be so heartless, so cruel?

He came across Aditya at the head of the staircase. Aditya inquired about his mother's condition and he seemed to be genuinely sorry for him.

'Have you heard the news?' he asked suddenly.

'What news?'Debadutta looked questioningly at Aditya.

'It is about our MD.'

'What about him?'

I don't know if it would be right to tell you about it in your present state of mind. It may hurt you. But I think you should be told.'

'Skip the suspense,' Debadutta said, 'and tell me.'

'Remember the investigative report you have prepared on one MLA who was sending some Sikh terrorists to foreign countries?'

'Of course!'

'Do you know why it has not been published till today?'

'It will be published soon,' Debadutta said casually. 'The MD says he will collect some more authenticating evidences to add to the news item before sending it for printing.'

'Authenticating evidence, My foot!!' Aditya returned scornfully. 'The deal has already been done.'

'Deal?'

'Yes, deal! Ten lakh rupees have changed hands. The investigating report and the supporting evidences like the CDs etcetera have been very conveniently dumped in the garbage bin. Didn't that MLA offer you a lakh of rupees for dropping the news? But you rejected the offer and insulted him. So he went for a direct transaction with the boss. You know the morals of our boss. That fellow is bringing out this newspaper only for earning money through blackmailing the big shots. Offer him a bribe of just a hundred rupees and he will grab at it without any compunction. That's why he is losing the elections repeatedly. It is all because he had incurred the ill will of people.'

Debadutta listened, disbelief and hatred in his eyes. The back of his ears felt hot. His heart was beating erratically. He recalled how hard he had worked on the news, and risked his life while doing the investigation. It had taken more than a month's gruelling effort to collect all the information and the evidences!

He had done a sting operation on the criminal activity

of a MLA allegedly involved in a crime of sedition. The MLA had links with a group that was sending Sikh young men abroad ostentatiously for higher education. Actually they were sent to foreign countries where to get trained in wielding firearms. Debadutta, putting his life in jeopardy had collected pictures and other evidences to expose the realities of the fig leaf job.

A few days after he had collected the news a correspondent from a national news channel had approached Debadutta with an offer of five lakh rupees in exchange of the evidences. Debadutta had wondered how that National Channel had come to know about the news while no one else except the MD and Debadutta himself had any knowledge of it. Later he learnt that the MD himself had leaked the information.

So, the old fellow is a master business man! He had made the deal for ten lakh instead of five! How disgusting!! Debadutta was filled with revulsion for the MD. He had sold away all the hard work Debadutta had done and all his efforts to expose seditious activity of the MLA for a mere ten lakh! There was nothing Debadutta could do except curse his own stupidity. The smouldering frustration and hatred inside him sparked off to a raging flame threatening to devour the whole of him. He returned to the hospital, his spirit scorched black.

Santanu was sitting by mother's bed, holding her hand in his own. Debadutta's eyes softened. Santanu had already given a bottle of blood to mother and ten thousand rupees for treatment. He had come to the hospital to give another bottle of blood. Debabdutta had asked him to remain in the hospital with mother while he went to the newspaper office to arrange more money. But, Debadutta thought bitterly, he had to return empty handed. Santanu, who worked in the post of Assistant Manager in a private bank, too was a good friend of Debadutta like Aditya and Swapnajit. It is because of these friends who extended unconditional help in this difficult strait, Debadutta thought gratefully, he could afford to get his mother proper treatment in a good hospital. His own office where he worked round the clock with all sincerity and dedication had left him in the lurch.

He looked at his mother. How old was she? May be in her early fifties! But she looked shrunken and pale. Her eyes had sunk into deep sockets, and her skin was badly creased. The disease had scraped all vitality out of her.

She opened her eyes and looked at Debadutta as if she could guess what he was thinking.

'You look so pale and drawn,' she said. 'It is because you have been moving around in the sun. Both of you go and have something to eat.'

Debadutta suddenly wanted to bury his face in his mother's chest and weep his heart out. He lowered his eyes afraid that mother might see the wetness in them.

'Ask the nurse here,' Santanu said, bringing him back to the harsh realities. 'The saline bottle is near about empty. She has to get a new bottle.'

Later as they sat together in the cabin, Santanu asked Debadutta whose turn was it to stay with mother that night.

'Don't you worry about that. I have applied for leave for two days. the chemotherapy will start from tomorrow. Mother will be in severe pain after the treatment. Only I can handle her in that condition. I will let you know if I need you here after the chemotherapy.'

Santanu patted his back. 'Whatever you say,' he said.

Debadutta was thinking if he should tell Santanu about how the MD had misused his investigating report and wheedled ten lakh rupees out of the MLA. Santanu's job as the Asst. Manager in a private bank was very demanding. He had to work under terrible pressure to meet the bank's monthly targets. 'The boss could be unbelievably rude if the targets are not achieved,' Santanu had told him once. 'There are times when I feel like committing suicide when I listen to the boss's tongue-lashings .'

Why to add to his worries by telling him of his own problems? Debadutta decided not to tell Santanu anything.

The call from the MD came unexpectedly next morning. Debadutta was busy in fulfilling the hospital formalities before the chemotherapy started. He touched the receive signal on his phone and the boss's voice came floating through to him in a loud rush.

'Where are you? Come and meet me in the office in half an hour.'

'I am on leave sir,' Debadutta said. 'The chemotherapy treatment of my mother will start today.'

'It is for your own benefit,' the boss returned. 'Meet me soon in the office,' the connection broke.

Debadutta completed the hospital formalities and hurried to the office. This time the peon Naik at the door of the MD's chamber did not ask him to wait and rather eagerly showed him in.

The MD too looked equally eager. 'Come in, come in,' he greeted him effusively as if he had been waiting for him. 'How is your mother?' he asked.

'Not good, sir. The chemotherapy will start today.'

'Don't worry,' the MD said sympathetically. 'Be positive. Things will come round.'

'Sir!'

'Every one of you is an asset to this establishment. You are all young, energetic , smart and capable guys. It is because of employees like you our newspaper has earned its position in the market.' The MD sounded almost genuine in his praise.

Debadutta couldn't believe his ears.

The boss took out a form from his briefcase and pushed it across the table towards him.

'What is this, sir?'

'Application form for a bank loan'

'Loan?'Debadutta looked startled.

'Don't get so worked up, Debadutta. Let me explain.'

'A bank loan amounting two and half lakh will be availed in your name.   but I will take the money. For the next five years a monthly instalment amount of seven and half thousand will be paid to the bank.'

'Seven and half thousand!'Debadutta exclaimed. 'My monthly salary is only four and half thousand…!'

'Silly! You won't have to pay anything. I will pay the instalment amount to the bank. Only the loan will be availed in your name. Our office is offering you a free insurance guarantee. God forbid, if something happens to you during these five years the loan amount will be waved. Your family will not have to take the responsibility of repaying the loan.'

'I don't get it, sir!'

'It is a simple arrangement. Why do you look so consternated? There is another advantage for you in this. You will get an advance of ten thousand rupees from this loan amount and only a thousand rupees will be deducted from your monthly salary towards its repayment.

Debadutta did not say anything.

'What do you take so much time for signing a simple loan application form? The MD said and laughed. 'Loans have been incurred in the name of all the staff members of the office. Some staff members have even availed more than one loan from different banks. They had no misgivings about the repayment. They rather volunteered to do so in the interest of the establishment. Why do you look so reluctant? How could you have a job security if the establishment runs in loss? You must take that into serious consideration. It is really unfortunate if you do not have this much loyalty towards the establishment where you earn a living.'

Several arguments in support of and against the MD's suggestion wrestled with one another in Debadutta's mind. With such a commitment he would be stuck in this office for the next five years. What if the MD or the establishment did not pay the monthly instalments to the bank? What if he got a better job offer in some other office in these five years? He couldn't resign the job here unless the loan amount is cleared.

'Why do you look so undecided?' The MD now asked in a raised voice. 'Can't you trust me? Am I your enemy that I would send you to the dogs? It is because I have spent a lot of money from the office account that I have to incur this loan in the name of different borrowers and return it to the account. I am not closing the establishment down. The newspaper will come out as it has been doing for years.'

'No sir, I was just thinking that how will the bank sanction a loan of such a big amount when my monthly salary is only four and a half thousand?' it was the only defence he could think of at that moment to prevent the boss from forcing him to take a bank loan.

'You need not have to break your head over that. I can make it forty thousand instead of four in the documents. The bank people are known to me. There will be no problem in obtaining a loan. You just put your signature as the applicant, take the advance of ten thousand rupees and take care of your mother's treatment.'

Debadutta could see no way to escape the boss's hounding eyes. He gathered up courage and made a last ditch effort to stall the act.

'I am taking it with me, sir. I will sign and return it to you tomorrow.'

'Do you want to consult an astrologer to spell out a propitious moment for signing the form?What is the problem in signing it now, here?' The MD was getting impatient.

Debadutta had nothing to say to that. He tried to judge the entire thing in a positive perspective. With ten thousand rupees he could afford another chemo for his mother. The only price he had to pay for it was his commitment to be with this office for the next five years. He would have to slave here and live through hell for the next five years. But his mother would survive for a few more days or months.

Five years of living death every moment here for him in exchange of an extension of five months or so in the life span of his mother!!

Seen like that, the deal did not look bad.

Debadutta made up his mind and reached out for the loan application form.

●●

Black Eagle Books

www.blackeaglebooks.org
info@blackeaglebooks.org

Black Eagle Books, an independent publisher, was founded
as a nonprofit organization in April, 2019. It is our mission
to connect and engage the Indian diaspora and the world at
large with the best of works of world literature published on a
collaborative platform, with special emphasis on
foregrounding Contemporary Classics and New Writing.

Lightning Source UK Ltd.
Milton Keynes UK
UKHW010438211122
412554UK00005B/381